UNDER SUSPICION

THE 12ᵀᴴ DETECTIVE INSPECTOR CAROL ASHTON MYSTERY

BY CLAIRE McNAB

THE NAIAD PRESS, INC.
2000

Printed in the United States of America on acid-free paper
First Edition

Editor: Lila Empson
Cover designer: Bonnie Liss (Phoenix Graphics)
Typesetter: Sandi Stancil

Library of Congress Cataloging-in-Publication Data

McNab, Claire
    Under Suspicion : a Detective Inspector Carol Ashton mystery /
by Claire McNab.
        p.   cm.
    ISBN 1-56280-261-5   (alk. paper)
    I. Title.
PS0000.00000   2000
813'.54—dc21

                                                                    CIP

For Sheila

Acknowledgments

My editor, Lila Empson, and typesetter, Sandi Stancil, are simply the best. And my deep thanks to proofreader Judy Eda. This book would not exist without their superlative skills.

ABOUT THE AUTHOR

CLAIRE McNAB is the author of twelve Detective Inspector Carol Ashton mysteries: *Lessons in Murder, Fatal Reunion, Death Down Under, Cop Out, Dead Certain, Body Guard, Double Bluff, Inner Circle, Chain Letter, Past Due, Set Up,* and *Under Suspicion.* She has written two romances, *Under the Southern Cross* and *Silent Heart,* and has co-authored a self-help book, *The Loving Lesbian,* with Sharon Gedan. *Murder Undercover* is the first Denise Cleever thriller. Look for *Death Understood,* the second Denise Cleever thriller, in the fall of 2000.

In her native Australia Claire is known for her crime fiction, plays, children's novels and self-help books.

Now permanently resident in Los Angeles, she teaches fiction writing in the UCLA Extension Writers' Program. She makes it a point to return to Australia once a year to refresh her Aussie accent.

PROLOGUE

Have you ever wanted to kill someone? When I was young I remember often being filled with silent rage, wanting someone to disappear forever, vanish in a silent puff of acrid smoke. Mostly, I just thought about it, fantasized how I would kill. My imagination was often violent — I smashed hands that had beaten me, tore out eyes that had mocked me, ripped out tongues that had derided me.

I never acted on these impulses, though, except for that one time, with Simon Shales. Of course, that could have been an accident. After all these years, I'm not sure myself. I certainly *wanted* him dead, but whether I really pushed him or he slipped and fell in front of the bus, isn't quite clear to me now. What is clear is how happy I was, how relieved that he had gone, and could torment me no longer.

Now, as an adult, I have the means, the will, and the guts to remove someone for sure. I'm plotting — how funny that sounds — murder. And I know I'll feel the same happiness and relief when it is all accomplished that I felt when the school bus turned Simon Shales into a bloody bundle of flesh and clothes.

I'm older and wiser, and I understand myself better, so I know this time I'll feel much more. Exultation, joy, and the sheer pleasure that comes from doing something well, of being smarter, quicker, and more powerful than everyone around me.

Wish I could tell them. They'd be shocked, amazed, dumbfounded. And admiring.

CHAPTER ONE

In the gray early light the Qantas jumbo jet circled over Los Angeles and then back over the ocean, waiting for permission to land at LAX. From her window seat Carol could see patterns of streetlights spread in an immense grid covering the floor of the mountain-ringed basin that held the city. A layer of smog smudged the air so that she could only just make out the tall buildings of downtown LA.

Sinking lazily toward the runway, the jumbo jet crossed over a fat freeway, five lanes of vehicles charging each way in an urgent flow that seemed to Carol to be like a dual artery of some enormous body.

"The Four-oh-five," Inspector Peter Karfer said with authority, craning over Carol to gaze out the window. He had a provoking air of superior knowledge, and Carol wasn't looking forward to spending the next few weeks in his company.

"Busiest freeway in the nation," he went on. "You can imagine what a bitch it was when the ninety-four earthquake broke its back in a couple of places. I was here then, you know. Holidays. Bit of a shock, the whole thing. Threw us clear out of the hotel bed. Afterward, Majorie didn't sleep for a week."

His smile, Carol thought, was meant to indicate that *he* had been undisturbed by the experience.

She made a vaguely affirmative noise, not wanting to encourage any further confidences. It wasn't that she actively disliked Peter Karfer — she didn't know him well enough — but rather that she found him tiresome. Their careers had run in parallel, and she'd met him on different occasions, but they had never worked together. Karfer had the reputation of being jovial and easygoing. Certainly he was affable, but she had

4

heard whispers of his propensity to take credit and shed blame, whilst knee-capping rivals who might get in his way.

She glanced over at Karfer as he sat back in his seat. He didn't look ruthless. In his forties, he had sandy hair cut very short, sharp blue eyes framed by gold-rimmed glasses, a full-lipped mouth, and a deep cleft in his chin. He smiled easily, had a deep, resonant voice, and, although obviously well educated, he cultivated a faintly larrikin manner to enhance his one-of-the-boys role.

Carol had never personally heard him say anything disparaging about female police officers, but she had a feeling that he didn't consider women his equals and that he was unlikely to be pleased if one was promoted over him. Karfer had already inquired, smiling, if Carol was intending to apply for promotion to chief inspector, and Carol, smiling in turn, had said she hadn't really thought of it — had he considered promotion himself? He'd lifted his shoulders and grinned. "I dunno. Maybe."

She hadn't been delighted to discover that both she and Peter Karfer had been accepted for an FBI program open to international law enforcement agencies and had been booked in adjoining seats on the same flight out of Australia. The police service had provided economy travel tickets, but Carol had sufficient frequent-flyer miles to upgrade to business class, so she would be assured, she thought, of a peaceful trip with a stranger sitting beside her. She wanted to avoid Karfer chatting away to her about work, particularly as her most recent high-profile case had had a less than desirable resolution, and she didn't want to give him the opportunity to have a sly dig at her about it.

Carol had said good-bye to everyone and boarded the plane a little early, settling into her window seat with two novels to read and the pleasant thought that for the next thirteen hours no phone would ring, no responsibilities would impinge.

She had scarcely taken a sip of the coffee the flight attendant had brought her when Karfer's cheerful voice said, "Great, isn't it, Carol? Thought I wouldn't have enough miles, but I just squeaked into business class. Then the guy next to you said he'd swap seats with me, so we could travel together."

He had the assured air of one who is confident of being always welcome. Carol repressed a sigh. "I hope you're not looking for conversation, Peter. I'm tired, and I'd rather not talk."

He ignored that. "Looking forward to the FBI? Should be quite an experience, I've heard. Actually know a couple of officers from the U.K. who are doing the course with us. Have you heard of Magic Mike of Scotland Yard?"

"No. Never heard of him."

Her flat, uninterested tone didn't seem to

register. "Chief Inspector Michael Yench," Karfer went on, "also known as Magic Mike because of the work he's done on antiterrorism. He came down hard on the IRA when they targeted London in the early nineties."

He looked at Carol expectantly. When she merely looked at him, he went on as though she'd queried him. "You want to know how I met him? First ran into Mike when he was out here a couple of years ago chasing up stuff on an IRA link with Australia, and then we met up again when I was in London a few months back. He's a big wheel in drug enforcement these days. For a Pom, Mike's not bad. Big guy, and a lot of fun. I'm sure you'll hit it off with him."

When Carol didn't respond he went on, "Maybe his offsider would be more your style. Debra Caulfield. Deb's tough as a bloke, but twice as pretty."

The *more your style* was said with subtle emphasis, and Carol felt a wave of vexation. "I can hardly wait to meet Magic Mike and Deb," she said caustically.

He peered at her. "You sound fed up. What's the matter?"

"As I said before, I'm tired and I don't feel like talking."

Plainly put out, he murmured "Righto" and turned his charm on the nearest female flight attendant. Then, after the several courses of dinner — served with real tableware and individual

7

tablecloths — Karfer became immersed in the movies showing on the personal screen, which popped out of the armrest between them, and so mercifully left her alone.

Carol had read for a while, then slept, the kaleidoscope of her dreams blending with the steady roar of the engines as they forged their way across the Pacific Ocean. She would swim up to wakefulness, then slide back into the procession of images: Mark Bourke grinning as he assured her that he wouldn't touch the paperwork in her in-tray; at the airport her son, David, his pale hair and green eyes mirroring hers, hugging her good-bye; Sybil kissing her cheek with neutral friendliness; Aunt Sarah squeezing Carol tightly and warning her, "Don't trust anyone. If I thought for a moment you'd listen, Carol, I'd beg you to call this trip off. I've seen a shadow in your future."

"Since when have you been a psychic?" Carol had chuckled, thinking Aunt Sarah had to be joking. It was strange for her aunt to recommend caution, as Sarah's personal motto had always been expressed as "Dare mightily!" and, when not engaged in ecological activism, she was an intrepid traveler.

Aroused from a confused dream where Aunt Sarah was just about to tell her details of the danger that faced Carol in the future, she found it was time for breakfast, Carol had sleepily swallowed scrambled eggs as she mentally prepared herself for Los Angeles. She was being met by an old school friend at the airport, so she crammed herself into the minuscule washroom just ahead of the rush and made efforts to make herself look presentable. Cleaning her teeth with the travel toothbrush and tiny tube of toothpaste thoughtfully provided by the airline, she considered her face in the unflattering glare of the lights over the mirror. The illumination, she thought, seemed designed to shake the confidence of all but the most attractive. She looked at herself critically. Carol had always taken her good looks for granted — she'd been, she'd always thought, lucky in the genetic draw, having inherited her mother's beauty and her father's slim build.

Heavy maintenance time coming up, she thought, inspecting the spray of fine lines at the corners of her eyes, the result of too many times of scorning dark glasses to squint in bright sunlight.

The engine note changed as the plane began to sink toward the land. Suddenly full of a pleasant anticipation, Carol went back to her seat. A new country, new people, new challenges to meet. On an impulse, she'd requested permission to attend the FBI Academy in Quantico, Virginia, a desire, she admitted to herself, to escape for a while from the demands and pressures of her job. And, if she were honest with herself, it was also because she needed to gain a breathing space, a time away

9

from everything familiar so she could gain a new perspective, not only of her career, but of her personal life.

Peter Karfer, freshly shaved and smelling of a light cologne, tightened his seat belt. "Take off and landing," he observed, "are the most dangerous times. Most crashes happen then."

"You're a comfort, Peter."

He grimaced at her. "Sarcasm will get you nowhere, Carol. I don't doubt we'll make it to the ground, one way or the other. I'm booked in the Airport Hilton. You?"

"I'm staying with a friend."

Karfer raised his sandy eyebrows. "I didn't know you knew anyone in LA."

"How could you?" Carol said shortly.

Her cool tone amused him. "I'm a detective, remember? You'd be surprised what I know."

She looked at him sharply. "Meaning?"

He spread his hands. "Meaning nothing at all."

The massive plane touched down so lightly it was a moment before Carol realized the wheels were on the tarmac. Then the roar of engines in reverse slowed them to a stately pace, and they began an interminable taxi to the terminal, which seemed located as far as possible from their point of landing. A cheerful warning admonished passengers to keep seat belts fastened until the plane had come to a complete stop at the arrival gate. "It's six thirty-five A.M. local time, and welcome to Los Angeles," added the chirpy voice.

Carol reset her watch, musing on the odd effect of the International Date Line, which zigzagged down the mid-Pacific to keep to open water, and which ensured that Carol was arriving in America on the same day that she had left Sydney, but several hours earlier.

Gathering his things from the seat pocket in front of him, Karfer said, "I'm spending two days here before flying to Washington to play tourist for a couple more before the course starts. You're welcome to join me anytime, but I suppose you'll be spending your time with your friend."

"I suppose I will." The exasperation she had felt at his probing was rapidly become an irritation.

He gave her a cheeky grin. "We Aussies have to stick together, you know. Strangers in a strange land, and all that. Besides, I get the impression the FBI types like to really test you, put you through your paces, and I reckon we'll need to be looking out for each other."

She was saved from any response by the ping as the seat-belt sign went off, a signal that was immediately followed by a wave of activity as passengers leapt from their seats to open overhead bins and collect their possessions.

Carol was expecting the worst from Los Angeles international entry, having been told many horror stories of long lines and imperious officials who amused themselves by making the whole process as difficult as possible. She'd conscientiously completed the immigration forms given to her in the plane, taking seriously the injunction that any carelessness in filling them out would result in long delays.

Prepared for a long wait, she was happily surprised to find that their flight's early arrival meant that there were no long queues, and in only a few minutes she was past the first entry point and, followed by Karfer, who kept up a running stream of comments about everything around them, heading for the luggage carousel. As they approached, a buzzer sounded and the mechanism ground into life.

Carol reflected that this could be any airport, anywhere. Passengers stood around waiting, with various degrees of boredom, anxiety, or fatigue, watching the suitcases as they were spat out of the metal mouth of the carousel to slide like helpless bodies onto a constantly circulating loop that took them around and around until an owner recognized an item and reached out to yank it from the display.

Carol's suitcase, marked with a red priority tag, was one of the first to appear, and she seized it before Peter Karfer could help, nodded to him, and set off for the final customs gates. She'd splurged on a new suitcase, the giant version of the small wheeled cabin bags, and it glided along behind her like some huge, black pet.

Another few moments, and she was painlessly through and walking up a slight incline that led arriving passengers into the waiting area of the terminal. Early as it was, there was a crowd, and a cacophony of different languages hit her as she maneuvered around a knot of people who had slowed to scan for friends and relatives.

Jill had insisted that it was no trouble to come to the airport to pick her up. Carol got out of the way of the stream of people coming behind her and looked around.

"Carol!" Jill del Bosco came bounding over, looking fresh and buoyant, as though it were not unconscionably early in the morning. They embraced, then stood back, smiling. Carol had only seen Jill a few times since her friend had left Australia to marry an American attorney six years ago, although they had kept in touch with birthday and Christmas cards and, lately, by e-mail. "You look tremendous," Carol said, meaning it.

Jill was tall and lean, with streaked blond hair, perfect red nails, and flawless makeup. She was wearing tight blue jeans, a pale rose cashmere sweater, and an indefinable air of privilege. She was thinner than Carol remembered, and her smile seemed whiter and brighter. Carol vaguely recalled Jill mentioning that cosmetic dentistry had been an anniversary present from her husband.

"I hope you're going to introduce me," said a male voice. Peter Karfer gave Jill the benefit of a warm smile that crinkled his eyes as he looked her over with approval. "Carol, this friend of yours is one stunning lady."

Jill's expression of disgust made Carol laugh. "Forgive him," said Carol. "We've just had a long flight."

"Since Carol obviously has no intention of introducing us, I'm Peter Karfer." He extended his hand. "And I'm sorry to say I haven't heard a thing about you."

She shook his hand briefly. "Jill Fontaine. Welcome to Los Angeles."

Carol looked at her curiously. Jill hadn't made a thing about keeping her own name when they married, and the return address on mail had always been Hal and Jill del Bosco.

"You're an Aussie? Damn it, I was hoping for an intro to a genuine California blonde." He put an arm around Carol's shoulders. "Sorry, Carol, but the Yanks do turn out the best blondes. Everyone knows that."

As Carol shrugged off his half-embrace, he said with mock alarm to Jill, "Next you'll break my heart by saying you're married."

"I'm afraid I am. Great to meet you, Peter, but we have to run."

"No problem." He hesitated, his face dejected. It was clear to Carol that he was hoping that Jill would come up with an invitation of some sort. "I'll be around for a couple of days . . ."

"There's lots to do in this town." Jill picked

up one of Carol's bags. "Sorry, but we've got to be going."

When Carol looked back, Karfer was staring after them, his face a cold mask. Carol felt a cold finger of disquiet, then shrugged to herself. If Peter Karfer was offended — too bad. It wasn't worth worrying about.

CHAPTER TWO

Jill waited until she and Carol stepped onto the pedestrian bridge leading to an ugly cement-gray parking structure before she said, "Well, *he's* a piece of work."

Carol glanced over at the crush of vehicles below. Raising her voice above the impatient revving of engines and blasting of horns, she said,

"You've just met Mr. Charm of the Sydney cops —
Detective Inspector Peter Karfer. Impressed?"

"And you're spending the next few weeks with
him? Rather you than me." Jill raised her key
ring, and halfway down the row of cars the lights
on a tomato-red BMW obediently blinked. "The
guy's getting a bit long in the tooth for that
boyish aren't-I-cute stuff."

"Seems to work for him."

Jill made a face at her. "This town's full of
cute guys who are younger and better looking
than Peter Karfer. I see them every day. He'll
have his work cut out to impress anyone here."

Carol smiled at her with affection. "You're
talking just like a native."

"Am I? I can't help it. Hal rubs shoulders with
the shakers and movers in the business — and
that word here means the entertainment business.
We have to know all the right people, belong to
the right country clubs." She gave an impatient
snort. "It's all a game, Carol. Look the part, and
you're in. As long as I stay thin, keep a moderate
tan, go three times a week to the most upmarket
gym, turn up for tennis with the right wives, and
generally play by the rules, life in the sun can be
pretty good."

"Doesn't sound to me like you enjoy it all that
much."

Jill shrugged. "I do, and I don't. It's nice to
get the best table in a restaurant, front seats to a
show, to mention Hal's name and have per-

sonalized service, not to mention a measure of groveling deference —" She broke off to strike a mocking pose. "What little Aussie woman wouldn't warm to a life in the fast lane with the rich and famous, eh?"

Hoisting her bulky suitcase into the trunk of the red BMW, Carol said, "I noticed you called yourself Fontaine."

"Identity crisis," said Jill lightly. "Truthfully, I use both names. I'm del Bosco when necessary, and Jill Fontaine when I'm just me. Hal, bless his soul, doesn't mind at all, or if he does, he's wise enough not to say so."

Forgetting that in the States the front passenger sat to the left of the driver, Carol went to the wrong side of the car. "You're going to drive?" asked Jill, grinning. "You're welcome to try, if you like."

"Some other time."

As Jill made her way past lines of cars and huge sports utility vehicles, Carol looked over at her friend's familiar face. She and Jill had met on their first day of high school, and even though they had grown apart in later years, their shared memories of school and university, of friends and experiences, had made a link between them that had grown thin, but never broken.

The sun was glaring down when they joined the traffic clogging Century Boulevard. It seemed to Carol that the light in Los Angeles was flatter and less nuanced than in Sydney, but she had to concede that this impression might be related to jet lag. As she fished in her bag for dark glasses, Jill, having apparently read her mind, said, "You going to be jet-lagged? I've got a bit of a party set up for tonight, and it'd be great if you lasted long enough to meet some of those famous people you hear about every day."

"I refuse to believe in jet lag," said Carol. "Besides, all I need is bright light to reset my internal clock, and I can see I'm going to get plenty of that."

She did a quick calculation: It was about three in the morning in Australia, and the next day. *This way lies madness*, she grinned to herself.

"Enjoying yourself already?" said Jill, glancing over at her.

"Just getting orientated. Now, exactly which famous people are you talking about?"

Jill turned right onto a ramp that indicated it led to the 405 North. "Robbie Zow, for one. No doubt his arrest was featured in the Aussie media."

"Front-page news. When a Hollywood star is accused of attempted murder, that beats global warming or the latest famine in Africa hands down."

"Cynic," said Jill, accelerating as she joined the freeway traffic. Magically a space opened up, and they joined the mass of commuters bound for work. "Robbie Zow is bigger than all those things, and don't you forget it. Hal's defending him, and the trial's set to start the day after tomorrow."

Without signaling, she drifted across three lanes of speeding vehicles. Carol winced, but nobody flashed lights or blew a horn. In fact, it seemed to be the norm to dart into any gaps without giving any indication. "Traffic's good today," said Jill. "Half the time you'll get stuck in a stop-go jam for miles."

"About Robbie Zow . . ." said Carol.

Jill squeezed a smile at her. "Thought you'd be interested. He and Davina Alcine will be at our place tonight."

Carol couldn't prevent a startled glance. "The girlfriend he ran down in his driveway?"

"Tut," said Jill. "Is *alleged* to have run down. Actually, he did aim his Ferrari right at her, and it's some kind of miracle she wasn't badly hurt. As it was, she got thrown over the top of the car and didn't go under the wheels."

"You make it sound so matter-of-fact."

"That's life. Robbie was under the influence of God-knows-what, but Hal will get him off. Davina had forgiven him before she got out of hospital." Jill shot Carol a wicked smile. "She's hoping to be wife number-three, but I don't like her chances."

"Next you'll be telling me she's a witness for the defense."

"She is. This is *so* LA. But for the unfortunate

fact that there were people who saw the accident who fell over themselves selling their stories to the media, it's likely Robbie wouldn't have even been charged."

Carol visualized Robbie Zow's instantly recognizable face. His latest movie was playing in Sydney, and he stared from press ads and billboards with that cocky, crooked smile that was his trademark. Zow was handsome, of course, but he had more than that — he had a carefree charm that contained a hint of darkness, as though, given the chance, he'd be a bad, bad boy. And Zow could act. Carol had seen him in several movies and admired his ability to totally inhabit the role he was playing.

"I suppose it's bad form to ask for an autograph?" she said, mock-serious, thinking how thrilled David would be if she came home with such a prize.

"Very bad form. What you're supposed to do is go along with the fiction that he's just an ordinary guy. Mind you, Robbie'll be very insulted if you don't show, however subtly, that you're mighty impressed to meet him."

Seeming not even to check for an opening, Jill changed lanes to the right and zoomed down an off-ramp signposted WILSHIRE BOULEVARD EAST. "We live in Brentwood. O.J. Simpson territory," she said, merging into a slower, thicker stream of vehicles on the surface street. "Parking is a nightmare, but Hal says it's worth it for the address."

Having only met Hal del Bosco when he'd been visiting Australia before his marriage to Jill, Carol was curious to see him in his home territory. Certainly his name was synonymous with very expensive, very public representation, usually for serious offenses that less well-represented clients might consider with consternation. Hal, however, had an enviable record with juries, and accounts of his famous clients' trials and subsequent acquittals frequently made the international news services.

The del Bosco house was, Carol was hardly surprised to find, a mansion. Set behind stone walls and wrought-iron gates, the tall white columns that framed the heavy front door irresistibly reminded her of *Gone With the Wind*. The circular driveway ran through gardens that bloomed luxuriantly, even in winter. "Our humble home," said Jill.

"I had no idea you lived in a manor," said Carol innocently. "Is there a butler?"

"No butler, but someone cooks for us. And my personal trainer, Greg, comes early most weekday mornings. I'm lucky to have him — he's much in demand. I put him off today, of course. I might be able to arrange a session for you, if you want one."

"Personal trainer?"

"You don't think I got this figure by accident, do you? And it takes a bloody lot of work to keep it, I can tell you." Jill pointed a finger at Carol.

"I've taken my mantra from Wallis Simpson: 'You can't be too rich, or too thin.' Now there was a woman born before her time!"

The housekeeper, a sturdy woman with a beautiful mahogany face and jet hair pulled back in a tight bun, came out to help with Carol's luggage. "Would you like Maria to unpack for you?" Jill asked.

Carol found herself faintly horrified that a stranger might do that for her. "I'll do it myself." She smiled at Maria. "But thank you."

"I forgot to tell you," said Jill as they entered the entrance hall, which was flooded with light from a skylight that threw into relief the gray marble floor and crisp white walls. "Hal has arranged a special guest for tonight, just for you. Someone from the FBI."

"You're kidding me. Who?" Carol had to laugh. "Not the director, surely?"

"No, not that that's impossible," said Jill. "Hal does seem to know almost everyone who's anyone. In this case, however, it's someone a bit lower in the ranks, though a senior agent. Her name's Leota Woolfe. And Carol, she's heard of *you*. Don't know if that makes you famous, or notorious . . ."

CHAPTER THREE

A long, hot shower restored Carol, and she willingly followed Jill around for a tour of the house, which was luxurious and beautifully decorated. But Carol couldn't imagine living there herself. The rooms, the house itself, were too large, too much a show place. There were several areas for entertaining, including a dining room that was large enough to host a fair-sized banquet, a billiard room, and a comprehensive gym furnished with the latest in exercise gear. Carol found one little sitting room that she liked. It was crammed with comfortable furniture, and it was the only room that looked really lived in. Jill shut the door on its less-than-perfect tidiness with the confession that it was her favorite hideaway.

It was seven-thirty the next morning in the Blue Mountains outside Sydney, so Carol called her Aunt Sarah to assure her that the plane had landed safely and that she was securely at Jill and Hal's. "Everything's fine, Aunt, so your premonition was just a bad dream."

"Just be careful, my dear. That's all I ask."

"I'm always careful."

Aunt Sarah's derisive snort traveled the ten thousand miles as clearly as if she had been standing next to Carol. "Sure you are," she said. "That's how, for example, you got your nose broken."

Reflexively, Carol ran a forefinger over the bridge of her nose. "That was at work, Aunt Sarah, and it came with the territory. While I'm here in the States I'm just doing a course, and nothing can happen to me while I'm at the FBI Academy. Their security will be as tight as a drum."

"Okay," said Aunt Sarah, clearly not convinced.

After Carol finished the call she joined Jill for a light lunch on the sheltered patio that ran along one side of the house. The ice cubes clinked as Jill poured iced tea into Carol's glass. "You don't like iced tea?" she asked when Carol made a face.

"It must be an acquired taste."

Jill leaned back with a sigh and surveyed the sunlit garden. "This is the life, don't you think? A leisurely lunch, conversation with a dear friend, and nothing to do for the party tonight except get in the way of the professionals running it . . ."

"I could grow to like it."

"Carol, I know you. You'll never relax for more than five minutes at a time." She fiddled with a fork. "You don't see much of Justin."

It was a statement, not a question, and Carol was mildly surprised. Jill, of course, knew Carol's ex-husband well, as they had all been in the same circle of friends at university, but she hadn't realized that they'd kept in touch. "I see him occasionally because of David, but mostly I deal with his wife, Eleanor. Why?"

Jill looked a little embarrassed. "I should've told you before, but Justin has stayed with us a couple of times when he's been passing through on business. He and Hal hit it off, of course, both being lawyers."

"I don't mind, if that's what's worrying you," Carol said, uncomfortably aware that she *did* mind. She had kept very few close friends from her earlier life, and those she had she was disinclined to share with Justin.

"Why did you bring this up?" she asked.

Jill shrugged. "I'm not sure — I thought I should tell you we'd seen him. It seemed unfair not to let you know."

In an unspoken agreement, the subject was dropped and they turned to other things that had happened in their lives since last they'd met on one of Jill's quick trips home. Carol talked about her son and his brush with the law over marijuana. "Good thing I've never had kids," said Jill. "I would have killed him."

"Believe me, I thought of it," said Carol.

After lunch, convinced that if she gave in and took a sleep during the day she would never reset her internal clock, Carol decided to take a look around Brentwood. "It's quite safe to be a pedestrian," Jill assured her, "though believe me, not everywhere in LA is."

Leaving Jill coping with final arrangements for the evening, Carol decided to head for the Brentwood shopping center, called, Jill told her, "the village." Late winter in Southern California was mild, as all she needed was a long-sleeved shirt.

As she strode along she was keenly aware that she wasn't wearing her subcompact Glock. It was ridiculous, but she felt exposed because she didn't have the little gun snug in its concealed waist holster. Of course there was nothing to fear in the bright sunlight of this privileged area, but she still felt unsettled without the security of a firearm.

Reaching the village, she meandered along, window-shopping and listening to the American voices all around her. She supposed there must be the same odd disconnect for Americans visiting Australia when they found themselves in a sea of Aussie accents.

Crossing the street nearly got her skittled, as she automatically looked the wrong way before stepping off the curb. The most fascinating thing was to wander through a supermarket, seeing familiar and unfamiliar brands, and, extraordinarily, a huge range of alcohol for sale next to mundane items like butter and milk.

She checked out the pet-food aisle, scanning the strange cans and wondering which ones Sinker would like. While Carol was overseas, her spoilt black-and-white cat was sharing Sybil's place with Sybil's ginger Geoffrey. This was no problem, as Sinker and Geoffrey knew each other well and, if not close friends, were at least tolerable feline acquaintances.

When Carol got back to the house a white van with discreet lettering indicating it belonged to an exclusive catering firm was parked in front of a cream Rolls. The vanity plates on the Rolls made clear that it belonged to DELBOSCO. Hal, sleek in a beautifully cut gray silk suit, greeted her at the door, shadowed by a compact young man wearing a black T-shirt and a scowl. "Carol," said Hal, "so wonderful to have you here."

He turned his head to the young man. "It's okay, Bruce. Carol's a top cop from Australia. I'll be safe with her."

Bruce looked at her with suspicion, then retreated several steps back into the hall, from which vantage point he continued to assess her.

"Bodyguard," said Hal. "It's embarrassing, but I'm caught up in something . . ." He grimaced. "Sorry, can't discuss the details. You understand."

"Of course I do," said Carol, intrigued.

She had always thought successful trial lawyers needed to cultivate a resonant, ringing delivery, but Hal's light voice had a disconcerting nasal twang. Otherwise, he looked the part: His thick black hair was carefully styled, his heavy features were tanned, his smile was warm and confident. He'd put on weight since she'd last seen him, and his heavy jaw was showing the beginnings of jowls.

He took one of her hands in both of his and squeezed it warmly. "You must promise me you'll treat everything as if it's your own."

"The Rolls too?" she asked, mischievous.

Hal del Bosco gestured expansively. "The Rolls too. Can I give you a lift? Is there anywhere you want to go?"

"No, no," she protested, laughing. "It's good to see you, Hal."

He put an arm around her and led her down the hallway, Bruce following closely behind them. "Jill says you can only stay two days. It's not enough, Carol. I do hope you'll be able to stop over in LA on your way back home after Quantico, but if you can't, we may be seeing you anyway. I have to be in Washington midway through next week. I'll be there for a few days, and the capital's not far from where you are in Virginia. Jill's talking of coming with me, so we can all get together."

"I'd like that. I haven't been a student for so many years, I suspect I'll need a lot of breaks to cope with the pressure."

Dropping his arm, he turned to her with a smile. "Speaking of the FBI, you know I've lined up Agent Leota Woolfe for tonight? She's in LA tidying up some loose ends in a case."

"Something interesting?"

"You could say that, but forgive me again — I'm afraid I can't discuss it at the moment."

"You're getting to be a regular man of mystery," said Carol with a grin. "Is the fact you need a bodyguard related to Agent Woolfe's loose ends?"

An almost imperceptible tightening of his features made her sure she was right, but he avoided answering by saying, "Leota is one of the many feds I know. Goes with my line of business. I've so many clients who will insist on running foul of the federal government in one way or another." He gave a bark of laughter. "Bless 'em," he said, making a sweeping gesture. "They've made all this possible."

A rotund middle-aged woman wearing a voluminous pink-and-black outfit that resembled loose pajamas opened the door they'd halted beside. "Excuse me, Hal, the senator's on the line."

"Be right there, Abby." He turned to Carol. "I think you'll like Leota Woolfe when you meet her tonight. She's very ambitious, very driven. My kind of person." He tilted his head to consider her. "Rather reminds me of you."

Carol frowned after him as he went into his study, followed by Bruce, who paused to look at Carol before he closed the door. Lately everybody seemed to be telling Carol that she was going to like somebody she was about to meet. Peter Karfer had assured her she'd like the couple of English cops who were doing the course, and now Hal was telling her she'd like Leota Woolfe. She almost felt inclined to dislike the lot of them on principle.

She found Jill in the cavernous, state-of-the-art kitchen discussing, with the import usually required for major surgery, the evening's menu and how it was to be served. The caterers, two slim men with earrings and attentive faces, listened and nodded reassuringly whenever Jill paused.

"Coffee?" she said to Carol, seeing her at the door. "Gary and Jon have it all under control, as usual, but I can't resist telling them how to do everything, no matter how hard I try."

The caterers gave Carol identical dry smiles. "It'll be a great success. Parties here always are," said one in a soothing tone.

"This time better not be an exception," said Jill. She grabbed two mugs, poured coffee, and took Carol into the adjoining, fern-filled sitting room. One wall was glass and overlooked the back area of the house. A blue-tiled swimming pool, encircled by graceful palms, scintillated in the sunlight. Its dazzling white surrounds held dark blue deck furniture shaded by blue-and-white umbrellas. There was an expanse of very green lawn, and then a red-surfaced tennis court.

Stretching out her legs, Carol sipped her black coffee. She felt relaxed, with no decisions to make and no responsibilities to shoulder. "I have a feeling you're going to tell me I'm going to like Robbie Zow," she said.

"Like him? You're supposed to *love* him. Actually, he's not a bad guy, for a star. Self-centered like all of them, but basically okay. It's easy to criticize, but I sometimes wonder how I'd be, if I were surrounded by people who told me I was wonderful, talented, and sexy as hell all the time."

"You mean people don't?"

Jill laughed. "Not that I've noticed."

Carol felt a small twinge of excitement at the thought of meeting Robbie Zow, and chided herself for it. "What do I wear?" she said, mentally checking through the wardrobe she'd packed. "How dressed up?"

"Anything goes. You'll see everything from jeans to Prada and Armani. Just be comfortable."

"I've met Bruce the bodyguard," said Carol, watching Jill's face.

Jill's mouth tightened. "I don't think it's necessary to have him here at home. It's an intrusion, and we have a full security system, but —" She broke off and shook her head.

"Are you worried Hal's in danger?"

"No, not at all. It's all because of the ridiculous flap over the Rackham case."

Surprised, Carol said, "Rackham? You mean the British minister who disappeared on a trip to the States?"

"The very one. Walked out of his Washington, D.C., hotel one afternoon three weeks ago and hasn't been seen since. His wife has retained Hal as her attorney. Seems she's under suspicion." She gave a snort. "Michele Rackham wouldn't be capable of plotting murder, or anything nefarious, if you ask me. You can judge for yourself — she'll be a guest tonight."

"So why would Hal need a bodyguard?"

A shadow of irritation crossed Jill's face. "I'm not altogether sure, and Hal won't discuss it. All I can say is the FBI, the CIA, and MI5 are all running around blaming each other because no one can find Sir Richard Rackham."

"Does Hal have any idea what might have happened to Rackham?"

"Oh yes," said Jill. "Hal seems to think he's dropped out of sight deliberately." She put up a hand to forestall Carol's next question. "Don't ask why. I've tried, and Hal just looks mysterious."

CHAPTER FOUR

By the time the guests started arriving that evening, Carol was feeling distinctly tired, and the thought of the bed waiting for her in the guest room upstairs was almost irresistible. She refused a glass of French champagne, thinking that it might finish her off altogether, and sipped orange juice instead, looking around to see if she recognized anyone. Jill and Hal greeted arrivals at the door, then funneled them down the hall to a huge room with French windows where waiters with trays of appetizers constantly circulated. Along one wall a full bar was manned by two bartenders, supplemented by a svelte young woman who topped off glasses as they were emptied.

Carol thought she could put names to a couple of the faces — one woman, Carol thought, was the head of a multinational cosmetic company, and she knew the tall man with the Vandyke beard as a lead actor from the cast of a long-running comedy series on television.

Everyone appeared to know everyone else, and as each new person appeared, he or she was greeted with warm cries. Several people smiled pleasantly at Carol, but no one spoke to her, and she began to feel she was in the middle of a movie where everyone had a script except her. She caught snatches of conversation, much of it puzzling, although now and then a name was mentioned that was familiar.

Her first glimpse of Robbie Zow surprised Carol. He was dressed casually, in a maroon turtleneck sweater and khaki pants. His face had the familiarity of an old friend, but on the screen he looked tall and substantial — and better looking. Reality was a different matter. His features were coarser, and although Zow was perfectly proportioned — his shoulders broad, his waist narrow — he was diminutive, and the woman clinging to his arm was even smaller.

Zow's luminous smile was much in evidence as he swam into a tide of welcomes, shaking hands energetically with the men, embracing the women. Carol stood back and watched. A lock of dark hair fell over his forehead in his trademark way, but his voice was less polished, more definitely accented, and Carol realized that when she saw him in movies he was assuming a neutral accent not his own.

"Come and meet him," said Jill, appearing beside her. "I call Robbie my pocket Adonis, but not to his face, of course."

Robbie Zow greeted Carol as though she were someone he'd been waiting all his life to meet. "You're an Aussie!" he exclaimed. "I love you people — so friendly, so welcoming. I've been on location in your wonderful country several times. Fabulous place."

His companion, crinkled golden hair, wide blue eyes, and swollen, bee-stung lips, clung to him as though he were a life preserver thrown into a stormy sea. "Hi," she said to Carol when she was introduced as Davina Alcine. She gave an assessing glance to Carol's black pants and green silk top, then checked out her jewelry, before looking into her face. "Hi," she said again.

Carol was tempted to ask for a score, but found it wasn't necessary, as Davina's attention slid away, clearly looking for worthier targets upon which to focus. Tugging on Zow's hand, she said in a breathy little-girl voice, "Honey, Howie just came in. We should say hello."

"Excuse me, Carol," said Zow, flashing his electric smile. "I'll take a rain check on our talk. Catch you later. You can count on it."

"Don't hold your breath," said Jill as they watched Davina pull him across the room toward a director so famous that Carol immediately recognized him.

Jill nudged her. "Although maybe in your case Robbie might be back, since he loves blondes, loves Aussies, and you fill the bill." With a grin, she added, "I'd watch out for Davina, if I were you. If she senses a rival, there is no telling what that woman will do."

"He's not quite what I expected."

Jill chuckled. "Disillusioned? As they say here, the camera loves him. Robbie looks bigger and better up there on the screen than ever he does in real life."

She took Carol's arm. "Here's Michele Rackham. Be a dear and keep her occupied for a few minutes while I check on the kitchen. I know everything's under control, but I have to look for myself."

The woman Jill introduced Carol to did not seem to fit the impression she'd gained earlier from Jill's comments. Carol had assumed that Michele Rackham would be pale and ineffectual, but this person didn't fit that description. Tall and rather bony, she wore a brilliant red suit. She had a high-cheeked, heart-shaped face that seemed too small for her decided features, her lightly graying, limp brown hair, and her resolute expression. "How do you do?" she said, as if she really meant the question to be answered.

"Fine," said Carol, taken aback at the preemptory, clipped, British tone. "And you?"

"Suppose you've heard about Richard? Everybody has."

"Yes. I'm so sorry." Carol felt at a loss. In her role as a cop she would radiate assurance as, solicitous but firm, she asked questions, probed responses for inconsistencies. In this situation she was like any stranger, stuck making polite conversation with someone to whom the unimaginable had happened.

Carol wondered if Michele Rackham loved her husband, if she lay awake at night with dreadful imaginings playing in her head. Or was she secretly relieved, pleased? And was she in a fog of uncertainty and fear, or did she know exactly what had happened? Where he was, dead or alive?

Michele Rackham leaned closer to Carol to say in a penetrating whisper, "The authorities are badgering me, you know, but I can't imagine what I'm supposed to have done with him. Can you?"

"I'm not sure what you mean."

"My husband," she said. "Disappeared into thin air." She unexpectedly grinned. "So inconvenient for everyone, but then, Richard never did care for anyone else's convenience."

By the final course of dinner, a meal that was quite as excellent as the caterers had predicted, Carol was so drowsy that she felt she could put her head down on the table and fall instantly asleep. It was not that the guests on either side were boring — she had Hal to her right and Darby Clegg, a renowned author of true-crime books, on her left, but she'd been tempted by the red wine, and although she'd sipped it sparingly, the alcohol was acting like a sleeping pill.

Robbie Zow had entertained the table with in-jokes about other actors, and his own experience of being stalked by middle-aged twins who had broken into his house and left loving messages in the pockets of his clothes. All the time Davina gazed at him adoringly, laughing appreciatively when he paused, and now and then casting a proprietary glance around the table as if to ensure that everyone understood that this man was hers.

Darby Clegg, lined and thin and with a sparse mustache and even sparser black hair, leaned over to whisper to Carol, "Zow's going to dump Davina as soon as the jury finds him not guilty."

"Really?"

"Really. You can take my word for it, I'm an expert. My next book is on stars and their run-ins with the law. *Hollywood Shenanigans*. What do you think of that as a title?"

Carol would have been diplomatic, but it wasn't required, as Clegg went on immediately, "My agent doesn't like it either. How about *Getting Away with Murder*? Does that grab you? Be honest, now." He shook his head gloomily. "Personally, I like *Evil Stars*, but my publisher won't hear of it."

Coffee was to be served in another room, so the moment Darby Clegg was distracted by the person on the other side of him, Carol took the opportunity to slip out the French doors and onto a marble balcony. She wasn't welcomed by darkness, as the garden was glaringly floodlit, but the chilly night air was bracing. Taking several deep breaths to clear her head before returning to the party, she couldn't resist doing a quick calculation of the time back in Sydney. Somewhere between three and four in the morning. No wonder her body clock was demanding that she go to bed.

Stifling a yawn, Carol was turning to rejoin the party when a voice said, "Surely we're not boring you?"

"Not at all. It's the jet lag getting to me, even though I refuse to admit it exists."

Leota Woolfe's teeth flashed in her dark face.

"You flew across half the world and arrived this morning? I'd call that an excellent excuse for fatigue."

She was trim and erect and had a direct gaze that was almost disconcerting in its intensity. There was a brisk, no-nonsense air about the black woman that was reflected in the navy blue dress she wore and the absence of any jewelry save for a square-faced watch.

The FBI agent had been late, arriving just before dinner was served, so, although Carol had been introduced to her, they had only exchanged a few pleasantries.

Carol said, "I believe you've heard of me. I'm curious to know how."

Leota leaned her elbows on the broad white edge of the balcony and gazed out at the floodlit garden. "You've worked on cases in Australia that had an international angle. For example, the FBI was involved with the CIA and Australia's ASIO on the American link to the Aussie Inner Circle terrorist group. In fact, I was personally involved at this end."

"And you remember me, although we never spoke to each other? I find that hard to believe."

Leota turned to her, grinning. "Such modesty. As a matter of course the Bureau runs checks on all international law enforcement personnel attending the Academy. Your name was flagged as having worked in liaison with the FBI, and I was interested enough to follow it up."

42

Carol frowned at her. "I don't understand why."

Leota shrugged. "It's one of the FBI's organizational initiatives to develop effective international police liaison. Your record is excellent, and the fact you're now involved in training at Quantico is a plus."

Raising her eyebrows, Carol said, "Am I supposed to go back to Sydney as some kind of plant for the FBI?"

The agent's hoot of laughter drew an unwilling smile from Carol.

"I'm surprised your superiors didn't brief you on this," said Leota. "The FBI is charged with detecting, investigating, and assisting in the prosecution of crimes committed against our citizens. Effective international police liaison is critical to carrying out this mission."

"Gosh," said Carol. "Do you always talk like a textbook?"

Leota chuckled. "Girlfriend," she said, "I think I'm going to like you."

CHAPTER FIVE

"Whatcha think?" Peter Karfer's voice boomed behind Carol. "Pretty impressive, eh?"

"It is that."

Bundled up against the penetrating cold, Carol and the other inductees to the special course, "Crime Fighting in the 21st Century," had just completed an orientation tour of the complex. It hadn't been snowing, but an icy wind blew off the upper reaches of Chesapeake Bay, and Carol had pulled up the collar of her quilted jacket and thanked the stars she'd had the foresight to bring her skiing gloves.

The FBI Academy, located on the United States Marine Corps Base at Quantico, Virginia, was a fabled place to Carol. She'd read about it in thrillers, seen it in movies, heard it referred to countless times in the media.

Thanks to the thoroughness of the FBI briefing, she now knew the National Academy Program had been founded in 1935, and from a tiny beginning had grown to a program with a worldwide reputation for excellence. The FBI Academy they were attending had been opened in the summer of 1972, and was situated on three hundred eighty-five acres of secured, wooded land that was also home the Drug Enforcement Administration.

One area she had heard about, and seen dramatized so many times, was Hogan's Alley, the famous training facility set up with facades representing the main street of a small town. It was used for training exercises that replicated bank robberies, night and day surveillance, kidnappings, and physical assaults. Carol remembered an instructional film she'd seen, where participants had to walk through the street, not knowing whether a criminal bent on murdering them or an innocent citizen would suddenly appear. The red-faced embarrassment of those trainees who blasted away at cutouts that represented young kids or harmless citizens was vivid in her memory.

Had she and her colleagues been enrolled in the standard eleven-week International Training Program for upper and mid-level law enforcement officers, Carol would have expected to have instruction at Hogan's Alley, but their small group of twelve were to experience a new, short personalized course devoted to the very latest developments in crime fighting, including the areas of forensic science, communications, interrogation techniques, and lethal and nonlethal weaponry.

Carol had originally applied for a specialist course detailing serial killer profiling, but her superiors had decided that both she and Karfer would gain greater benefit from the new course.

When he had first spotted her, Peter Karfer had greeted her like his long-lost relative, and attached himself firmly to her side while an admirably efficient instructor took their group through the facilities the Academy offered. Now that they were back at the assembly, a room heated almost to the point of being uncomfortable, Karfer said, "Back in a mo," and left her alone.

Carol looked around at the people with whom she'd be sharing the next few weeks. Earlier, when identification tags were distributed, Carol had noted there were cops from Canada, Britain, the Philippines, Scandinavia, Hong Kong, New Zealand, and Australia.

She was about to strike up a conversation with a large, Nordic man who looked the part of a civilized Viking, when Karfer returned, two people in tow.

"Carol, let me introduce Magic Mike and Deb, the Pommies I told you all about." Karfer made a sweeping gesture in Carol's direction. "I give you Inspector Carol Ashton, the best-looking cop in Sydney."

The way he subtly shaded the last phrase made it clear, at least to Carol, that he meant this compliment sarcastically.

Neither Mike Yench nor Debra Caulfield reacted to the mildly insulting term *Pommie*. In turn they shook hands with Carol, each clearly assessing her as they did so.

Chief Inspector Mike Yench was a big man in every way. He towered over Carol, his shoulders were massive, and his thick body and solid thighs strained the faded denim of his shirt and jeans. He had heavy features and a red, full-lipped mouth, and his reddish hair was crew-cut. For such a big man, his handshake was suprisingly flaccid and moist, and Carol found herself resisting the impulse to wipe her hand after he slowly released it.

Yench's voice had a touch of cockney. "These Yanks will be saying you and me come from the same place," he said. "They can't tell an honest Englishman from an Aussie, and have no idea it's as bad as calling a Yank a Canadian."

Sergeant Debra Caulfield was a slight figure next to her oversize companion. She had a cool, watchful manner, with a thin, intelligent face, firm mouth, and eyes so dark brown they were almost black. Her cap of glossy dark hair was cut for convenience, not style. She didn't speak, but just nodded to Carol, permitting herself a small movement at the corners of her mouth. Carol wondered if that faint grimace passed as Debra Caulfield's usual attempt at a smile or if, for some reason, the London officer was already indicating that she didn't like her.

"Deb and Mike are crash-hot operators," said Karfer to Carol, speaking as though he were personally responsible for their excellence. "Drugs, terrorism — you name it, they're on top of it." He grinned at the objects of his praise, "I reckon you two have come here to show the colonials how to do it, eh?"

Debra Caulfield gave an almost imperceptible shrug; Mike Yench said, "You talk too much, Pete. I've noticed that before. Not a good quality in a cop."

Karfer flushed, and Carol almost felt sorry for him. "Yeah, well," he said. There was an embarrassing silence, then Karfer looked across the room as if he'd seen something important, mumbled "Excuse me," and hurried away.

Looking after him, Yench said to Carol, "You and Pete good friends?"

"We're colleagues."

Carol's cool answer amused him. "I'd say you find Karfer a prick, like I do."

"He speaks very highly of you, too," said Carol.

Her dry tone brought an open laugh from Mike Yench. "You and me, Carol," he said, "are going to get along just fine."

Debra Caulfield's expression hadn't changed, but Carol felt a chill of dislike as the woman flicked a glance over her. "Karfer can be a right pig," she said.

These were the first words Carol had heard from her, and she was struck by her crisp, British accent that indicated, Carol thought, the upper ranks of British society, even though the sentence did not.

Further conversation was stalled by an announcement that additional admission procedures were to be completed before the evening meal. When she could escape, Carol went to the dormitory to spend some time alone before dinner.

She looked around the utilitarian room. There were six beds, and it was comfortable enough, but she was already missing the sound of kookaburras laughing and the tang of eucalyptus gums drifting through her bedroom window. Carol hadn't slept in a group situation since she'd been a trainee constable, and she wasn't altogether sure that she would endure the experience with equanimity. There were several Academy courses running concurrently, so the accommodation was full, and each small dormitory room had its full complement.

After inspecting the bathroom, which was illuminated by the most unflattering flat glare, Carol sat on the edge of the bed on which she'd dumped her luggage to study the map that had been included in their orientation folder. The main training complex had administrative offices, three dormitory buildings, a dining hall, a library, a classroom building, a large auditorium, a chapel, a gymnasium, and an outside running track.

She located Hogan's Alley. Nearby was a pursuit-and-defensive-driving training track. Firearms training was clearly important to the FBI, as apart from an indoor range there were an astonishing eight outdoor firing ranges, four skeet-shooting areas, and another range specifically devoted to rifle fire.

She turned to the class schedule, thinking how she had to admire the FBI's talents in organization. Everything was clearly set out, time was tightly allocated, and no participant need ever be hazy about when and where to report. This was, she thought, going to be an interesting experience, if not a comfortable one. As she unzipped her suitcase, Carol's thoughts turned to Leota Woolfe, who had said that she'd be seeing Carol at Quantico. The agent, Carol was sure, had been less than forthcoming when Carol had talked to her at Jill and Hal's party. Carol didn't imagine for one minute that the reason so much interest had been shown in her had anything to do with the FBI building bridges to international law enforcement bodies. She suspected that it was something related to Hal del Bosco's involvement in the Rackham disappearance, though how and why was more than Carol could fathom.

Sir Richard Rackham was a British politician with a reputation for impetuous actions and intemperate pronouncements, and his sudden disappearance had created intense media interest. There were no hints that espionage was involved, and a close examination of his past connections had turned up nothing that would indicate that he was a particular target, although he had been notable in his condemnation of violence in Northern Ireland and had on numerous occasions attacked the IRA for bombings and assassinations in British territory.

Carol could visualize Sir Richard's face as she had seen it in newscasts. He was in many ways the epitome of a certain sort of British gentleman who had appeared in cartoons over the years: He was corpulent and red faced, his intense blue eyes squinting a challenge to the world. He had a luxuriant white mustache, carefully tended. His hair, obviously fair when he was young, was now thin and bleached with age, and combed defiantly across his skull. When he spoke, he swallowed his words in the manner of the very upper class, his nasal tones loud and provoking. In the order of his interests, he had supported fox hunting, condemned immigration, and totally opposed any political union with Europe.

His sudden disappearance had activated media imaginations, and his fate had variously been seen as the work of the Irish Republican Army, one of many Middle East nations — Rackham had denounced most of them at one time or another — or even the CIA. This last theory was floated by the British newspapers, who ferreted out that Sir Richard was operating as a special envoy for the Prime Minister on some issue of national importance when he had vanished. Other explanations included that a mugging had gone wrong, that Rackham had engineered his own disappearance — sightings had been reported in the Bahamas, Canada, and Brazil — or that he was a victim of amnesia and was wandering around unaware of the huge efforts being made to find him.

"I see we're sharing the same room," said Debra Caulfield from the doorway, her tone showing no pleasure in the fact.

Carol smiled at her. "Is it that you don't like Aussies, or is it me?"

With a reluctant smile in return, Debra said, "Sorry. I have been a bit a pain in the neck. The fact is, I didn't want to be here in the first place."

"Then why did you apply?"

"It was nothing to do with me. I was told I was doing the course, and that was that." She moved to sit on a bed near Carol's. "So was Mike, but he doesn't mind."

"Have you any idea why?"

"Professional development," said Debra wryly. "What other reason could there be?"

Carol lingered unpacking and came late to the evening meal. The dining hall was like every facility designed to feed large numbers of people. It was designed to be easily cleaned, which meant surfaces that bounced sound and created a background of constant noise. There were queues of diners waiting to collect their food, while diners who'd collected their meals circled with laden trays looking for somewhere to sit.

"Come and join us," said Mike Yench, who'd commandeered a table. Carol would much rather have found somewhere by herself, as she was sure by the end of the course she would be heartily sick of his company, but she nodded, smiling, and slid onto a seat.

He made the introductions: "Everyone, this is Carol Ashton all the way from Sydney, Australia. Carol, I'd like you to meet Ian Forteys, Lars Svenson, and Nikki Lee, who's from Hong Kong. Deb and Pete you know already."

The cold weather had sharpened Carol's appetite, so she ate steadily and listened to the conversation around her. From the cadence in his voice, it was clear that Ian Forteys was Scottish. His hair was very dark, and he had clear, white skin that showed the shadow of his beard. He was very thin, with hollow cheeks and narrow, long-fingered hands. He both looked and sounded pleasant and easygoing, although Carol suspected that it was the Scottish burr in his voice that was disarming her.

Next to him was the Viking-like figure she'd been about to speak to when Peter Karfer had interrupted with introductions to Mike Yench and Debra. Lars had thick, yellow hair, a darker red-blond beard, and a strapping build. His voice was a low rumble, and his blue glance was piercing. It wasn't difficult to imagine him, ax in hand, standing at the prow of a Viking warship.

Sitting at the other end of the table was Nikki Lee, a substantial Asian woman with a wide, humorous mouth and a chuckle that made others smile. She'd been educated in England and spoke with an incongruous British accent, fully as plummy as Debra Caulfield's. Peter Karfer was sitting next to her, and his comments obviously amused her, as every few moments a shout of laughter came from her direction.

Mike Yench, showing none of his previous animosity toward Karfer, joined in, his deep laugh a bass line to Nikki Lee's soprano giggle.

Predictably, Debra Caulfield wasn't amused. She sat beside Yench, picking at her food. Carol thought she looked irritated, jumpy, but then, observing her, Carol had a sudden insight — it wasn't edginess that Debra was showing, it was anxiety, perhaps even fear.

CHAPTER SIX

The classroom was modern and soundproof, but the fact that it was warm pleased Carol the most. After a surprisingly good night — she'd clambered into bed convinced she'd never be able to sleep soundly in a room with five other people, the last thought she'd have before morning — Carol had gone on an early morning run on the outdoor track. She'd come back inside frozen to the core. Even a hot shower and breakfast hadn't managed to entirely thaw her out.

She thought ruefully that she was born for temperate climates. She'd skied in Australia, but the snow fields covered only a small area, and she'd dressed appropriately. She'd packed warm clothes suitable for the mild Sydney winter, plus a ski jacket and gloves, but two days of frosty Virginia had showed her it wasn't enough. The cold here seemed more biting, more vicious, and she made a mental note to buy a warmer jacket and pants at the first opportunity.

Looking around, she mentally checked off the faces of her eleven colleagues. All looked rested and ready to go, even Debra, who'd unbent enough to chat to Carol at breakfast. The other women in their room where pleasant and considerate, with the exception of one bumptious woman, a new arrival who had spread her possessions around without any thought for anyone else. She had the bed next to Debra, and had dumped half her considerable luggage on Debra's bedspread.

There'd been the makings of an unfortunate confrontation when Carol, in full conciliatory mode, stepped in and soothed everyone. Carol had smiled to herself at the time, thinking how her Aunt Sarah would hoot to see her so agreeable. Her actions weren't entirely without self-interest: She was curious about Debra Caulfield and interested in why she had spoken so disparagingly about Peter Karfer.

"All right, people," said the instructor at the front of the room, "I'd like your attention here to the front, please."

He swept them with a narrow look, then flipped some pages on the lectern in front of him. After clearing his throat, he began, "As part of our examination of new developments in interrogation, we will be looking at a sometimes ridiculed device, the polygraph or lie detector." He cleared his throat again, "The lie detector is not well named, as its purpose is not to establish beyond any doubt that a subject is lying, but only that, all things considered, the preponderance of evidence is that the subject is, or is not, telling the truth."

He had a flat, nasal delivery that Carol found irritating. She tried to concentrate on what he was saying and ignore his voice as he droned on. "Although refinements have made this instrument much more reliable in the detection of lying, generally test results are not accepted as evidence in United States courts, or, indeed, courts in other countries."

"That's because it's all bloody mumbo jumbo," said Peter Karfer, just loud enough for the instructor in interrogation techniques, Frank Vertelle, to hear.

Vertelle's jaw tightened. "Please leave any questions or comments until later, Karfer."

The FBI instructor looked hungry, thought Carol, but not for food. Physically he wasn't thin, like Ian Forteys, but his face was narrow and composed of sharp angles. His glance darted everywhere, constantly checking, probing, and assessing. He wore a dark suit, a white shirt, and a red tie tightly knotted. Irresistibly, he reminded Carol of a jackal, ever on the alert for some prey that might show weakness, so he could launch a successful attack and tear it to pieces.

This fancy made her smile to herself, a smile that disappeared when Vertelle said, "Something amusing you, Ashton?"

It was his custom, he'd said when he'd introduced himself, to call everyone, male or female, by his or her last name, baldly, with no salutation. "So we're to call you Vertelle?" Nikki Lee had asked.

"*Agent* Vertelle," he'd snapped.

The instructor was still waiting for a reply. Carol looked at him with dislike. "I'm not amused at the class," she said, adding with a small grin, "How could I be?"

He gave her a long, hard look, but obviously deciding not to carry it further, he continued. "The concept of the lie detector is based on the belief that a subject's body responds differently when the subject is lying than when telling the truth, although I must caution you that valid results do depend upon the tester and the framing of the questions."

He paused, then said with a waspish note and a glare in Peter Karfer's direction, "Each of you will have the opportunity to be tested on the very latest computer-enhanced lie detectors, and can judge for yourself the efficacy of the machine. You will see that a battery of results are fed into the computer program for evaluation — blood pressure, pulse rate and pattern of breathing, electrical changes on the skin, and voice frequencies. In addition, the very latest development in the detection of lying has been incorporated — a separate computer program that classifies forty-six muscle movements that account for the entire range of human expressions."

Vertelle tapped something on his lectern, and the screen behind him sprang to life. "The Salk Institute in California first developed this system to read the ever-changing micro-expressions on a human face and to draw conclusions about the emotions underlying these subtle twitches."

The short instructional film was fascinating. Some of the facial movements were so fleeting that it was only with slow motion that they could be seen. Carol watched as a subject, in normal time, seemed to be answering a question with a frank and open smile, then, replayed slowly, the almost infinitesimal beginning of a scowl was shown to flicker across his features, followed immediately by what was now clearly a false smile.

"Watch the eyes," said Vertelle, freezing the

screen using a laser pointer to indicate the corners of a woman's eyes as she smiled. "A true smile crinkles the eyes in a pattern that a computer can recognize. A lying smile creases the skin around the eyes into crow's-feet, not laughter lines, and the muscles of the face are tighter."

"This is a great help," rumbled Mike Yench with heavy sarcasm. "From now on I'll have the villains I nab laughing like fools so I can tell if the bastards are lying or not."

There were some amused sounds, but Frank Vertelle didn't seem to have a sense of humor. "That won't be necessary," he said. "The program is designed to detect all small variations in expression, not only smiles."

He blanked the image and turned to the class. "We'll see a live demonstration next." He nodded to a woman sitting quietly to one side. "We'll be using a Bureau expert, so it'll be next to impossible to fool the system."

"But a lie detector can be beaten, can't it?" asked Ian Forteys. "Even this micro-expression stuff?"

"Possibly by a very skilled actor, or a sociopath," Vertelle reluctantly conceded.

He shifted his glance to Carol. "Ashton, you can be our first subject. You look like someone who could lie convincingly."

The comment had an edge to it, and Carol felt the same baffled annoyance she had in school when she'd been the victim of a snide remark

61

from a teacher. However, she complied without demurring, going up to the front where the tester was setting up her equipment.

A voice from the door said, "All police officers should be able to lie convincingly. It's a job requirement." Leota Woolfe came into the room. "I'm here as an observer," she said.

Vertelle inclined his head. "This is Agent Woolfe," he said. His tone was neutral.

Carol's lips twitched. *I don't need a micro-expression program to read you,* she thought. *You don't like Leota Woolfe, and you resent her observing your class.* It was juvenile, she knew, but Carol couldn't help feeling pleased at his displeasure.

Leota Woolfe took Vertelle to one side and spoke to him softly. Carol's saw his eyes narrow. "Why?" he said.

The agent said something more, and Vertelle, frowning, nodded. Raising his voice, he said, "Ashton? You're off the hook. Caulfield, up to the front, please."

Debra Caulfield got to her feet with every evidence of reluctance. "I'd rather not, if you don't mind."

"It won't hurt. Hurry up, please."

Carol saw Leota hand the tester a page, then bend over her, obviously giving instructions. The tester scanned the material she'd been given, then, eyebrows raised, looked up at Leota. The agent gave her a firm nod, then moved away to the side of the room, where she stood, arms folded.

Lie detectors had no validity in Australian legal proceedings, but Carol had seen them in movies and documentaries and had heard stories how they had been beaten by mimicking guilty responses to innocuous questions.

Nikki Lee was obviously thinking along the same lines, asking, "Isn't there some way to confuse the lie detector, Agent Vertelle?"

"The best you can do is have inconclusive results," said Vertelle. "An individual can try to beat the system by flexing muscles or holding his breath, or even dosing himself with drugs or alcohol, but such countermeasures have very little success when the tester is well-trained and experienced."

The equipment was much less bulky than Carol had expected, comprising a small camera, a printer, and a portable computer. With deft economy, the tester attached various leads to Debra Caulfield, including straps to measure her breathing rate at both chest and stomach.

"Note," said Vertelle, "that readings will be taken to measure not only the rate of respiration, but also the pattern of deep or shallow breathing. In addition, the machine will analyze the subject's galvanic skin conductiveness, blood volume, pulse rate, and facial movements.

"Your name is Debra?" said the tester once she'd checked everything to her satisfaction. She peered into the screen of the laptop computer's screen as Debra responded affirmatively.

This harmless question was the first of two categories of questions. In a pretest interview, control questions that had no emotional charge and were demonstrably true were used to establish the normal parameters of a subject's response. Once established, then questions relevant to a specific incident or crime were asked, and the subject's bodily readings were recorded and compared to the control responses.

After a series of innocuous questions, each asked in an uninvolved tone, the tester paused and checked the page Leota Woolfe had given her. "Have you ever stolen anything in your life?" she asked.

"In my whole life? Of course I have."

Carol found herself nodding. This was the appropriate response, as it could be predicted that almost everyone has at some point stolen something.

There was a pause, then the tester asked, "Is Richard Rackham dead?"

Carol heard a sharply indrawn breath behind her. At the front of the room, Debra was standing, pulling the wires from her skin and shedding the straps around her body.

"I'm not going on with this," she said. Without meeting anyone's eyes, she stalked out of the room.

"Bloody hell," said Karfer. "What was *that* all about?"

At lunch Ian Forteys grabbed the seat next to Carol. "What do you think was going on with that black agent? What was her name? Woolfe?"

"Leota Woolfe."

He gave her a keen look. "You've met her before?"

"Yes, I have."

"Professionally?"

Carol considered the question. "In a way," she said.

Forteys beamed at her. "Getting blood out of a stone would be easier, I imagine, than interrogating you."

Carol made a face at him. "I don't know anything, so interrogation won't get you anywhere."

He inclined his head in Debra Caulfield's direction. Mike Yench was sitting next to her, his face close to hers as he spoke in a low voice. "What about her? Think she knows something about Sir Richard's abrupt disappearance?"

Carol looked over at the British officer. Debra's face was stone, her shoulders tight. Since sitting at the table she'd said nothing, eaten nothing from the plate in front of her. She even seemed impervious to Mike Yench's words. "She didn't want to answer any questions on the topic; that's all I can say."

Forteys's thin face was intent, and a faint flush showed clearly on his pale skin. Carol wondered why he was so stimulated by what had happened.

He said, not taking his eyes from Debra Caulfield, "She was set up this morning. Quite an effective ambush. I wonder what the next questions would have been, if she hadn't bolted."

Carol, motivated by the same curiosity, had taken advantage of the confusion that followed Debra's exit to go to the front of the room in an attempt to get a look at the questions Leota had handed the tester, but the agent had been too quick, snatching up the page and folding it several times before putting it in the pocket of her jacket.

"I'll speak with you later," Leota had said to Carol in a voice too low for anyone else to hear.

Remembering that confiding tone, Carol looked around, wondering if Leota was somewhere in the dining room. She became aware that the Scotsman beside her was using the same tone as he said softly, "I know a lot about Debra, and not all of it's good. She and Magic Mike make quite a team, but they cut corners, bend the rules, and there've been a few unexplained deaths on their patch. Even up in Edinburgh we've heard the rumors."

"Heard what?"

"They're cozy with informants — that's par for the course in drug enforcement, of course — but there's been a whisper around for years that it's not too healthy to get involved with them if you're going to grass on someone."

"Have you got anything specific?"

He shook his head. "Nothing that would stand up in court." Ian Forteys's grin had malice. "I've got to give it to them, they're Teflon-coated, at least up until recently."

Carol said, "I get the feeling there's something personal here, for you."

The flush under his white skin deepened. "You think that, do you?"

"It's my impression." She waited, her glance locked with his.

He looked away first. "Debra and I have some history. We dated when we were young constables together in London, but I went home to Scotland and she stayed where she was. Wasn't much to it then, and there's nothing to it now."

He rubbed his forehead. "She saw Mike Yench was going places, so she hitched her career onto his, and it paid off."

His tone was carefully neutral, but Carol sensed a vein of bitterness underneath. She said, "So what's the link to Sir Richard Rackham?"

"Rackham was a big antidrug crusader. Had wonderful PR. Questions in parliament, chairman of a keep-the-kids-clean organization — you name it, he was there as long as the media turned up, too. And, as a matter of course, he got to know the cops on the street."

Forteys paused. "You notice, Carol," he said, "how easy it is to refer to Rackham in the past tense?"

"You think he's dead?"

"I know he is," said Forteys.

CHAPTER SEVEN

Leota Woolfe caught up with Carol as she walked to the afternoon class. "Come with me."

Ian Forteys, coming up behind them, said with mockery, "Don't be late for class. Agent Vertelle will make you sit in the corner."

Carol grinned at Leota. "You'll get me into

trouble," she said. "I've already rubbed Agent Vertelle the wrong way."

"I'll write you a note."

She took Carol into an anonymous office furnished simply with a desk and filing cabinet. Shutting the door, she said, "Judging by your intense conversation with Forteys at lunch, I imagine you've already discovered the connection between Debra Caulfield and Sir Richard Rackham."

"We were under surveillance?"

Leota grinned at Carol's displeasure. "Couldn't keep my eyes off you," she said.

"Indeed?" Carol kept her face blank, wondering if this was arch humor or if the agent was actually flirting with her.

"Indeed. And I was interested in the conversation between Caulfield and Yench, too."

"I'm surprised," said Carol dryly, "that you didn't have directional microphones in place to record everyone's conversations."

"It's a pity we didn't," said Leota with every evidence of regret.

Frowning, Carol said, "Am I being set up for something? It feels like it."

"Not really. I'd just like you to keep your eyes and ears open."

"For what?" She didn't hide her impatience.

"Let me level with you."

"That'd be nice."

Leota grinned again at Carol's ironic tone, then her face grew serious. "When Rackham vanished, the FBI was called in because it was assumed he'd been kidnapped. He'd been complaining of being followed in London, and when he arrived in Washington, we worked with his people to vet his hotel room and make sure there were no weak spots in his security coverage."

"There clearly *was* a weak spot."

"Not exactly. It looks like Sir Richard gave his bodyguard the slip deliberately."

Carol thought of Michele Rackham's censorious attitude toward her husband. "Why is Michele Rackham a suspect in the disappearance?"

"To say she's a suspect is too strong, but she does seem to have purposefully engaged her husband's bodyguard to give Rackham an opportunity to slip away."

To Carol, it didn't seem enough to justify the FBI's close attention. "For that reason she's engaged a high-priced lawyer to look after her interests?"

"It's very possible Michele Rackham's interests run to something more serious. What do you know about Sir Richard?"

"More than I ever intended to know," said Carol tartly, "but I can see you intend to enlighten me further."

"Did Forteys tell you Rackham is very involved in the antidrug efforts in Britain?" When Carol nodded, Leota went on, "In fact, he's built his political career on the fight against illegal substances."

"Don't tell me," said Carol, having had her share of arresting hypocrites who denounced the very crime that they were secretly committing. "Rackham was involved in the drug trade himself. Yes?"

"Ecstasy," said Leota. "Ever tried it?"

"No."

Leota gave her a quizzical look. "Perhaps you should," she said.

Karfer patted the empty seat next to him. "Over here," he hissed.

Agent Vertelle glared from the front of the room as Carol sat down. "So nice that you could join us," he said with sarcasm. "We've been discussing advanced interrogation techniques. You'll need to catch up in your own time."

"Where've you been?" asked Peter Karfer as soon as Vertelle resumed his lecture.

"I was just delayed, Peter."

His gaze was curious. "Something to do with Deb, was it?"

"Let's talk later," she said to shut him up.

He nodded, satisfied. "Righto."

Carol had no intention of chatting with Karfer, but when the class stopped for a coffee break, he cornered her. He gestured toward Debra and Mike Yench, who were standing silently together. Debra looked exhausted, and Yench annoyed. "Something's up. I tried to talk to Mike and Deb, but they pissed me off."

Carol took a gulp of her coffee. It wasn't bad, she had to admit. In fact, it was a considerable improvement on the black tar that she drank every day at work. She had a sudden vision of her office — the hum of conversations, the phones ringing, the sense that something was always happening. Of course it would all go on without her. Victims would be killed, witnesses would be interrogated, the thread of truth under all the details would be, hopefully, revealed. She had a sudden pang of homesickness, wishing that she were there, consulting with Mark Bourke, watching with almost maternal pride as Anne Newsome grew in professional skills . . .

She became aware that Peter Karfer was still talking. "Sorry?" she said.

"Rackham — that's the name that put Deb into a tailspin this morning. You know who he is, I suppose."

"The British politician who disappeared," said Carol with a shrug.

Karfer sighed. "Come on, Carol. Something's going on here, and you're in on it, so be a good mate and tell me all about it."

"Tell you about what?" Mike Yench loomed over them. Carol thought how physically intimidating he was, not just because of his bulk, but because he stood too close. She didn't move, but she noticed Karfer backing up.

She said, "We were discussing this morning's session."

Yench grunted, then said to Karfer, "Get me a coffee, will you, Pete. Black, two sugars."

Karfer hesitated, then acquiesced, his face faintly flushed. Yench watched him go, then said, "Got plans for the weekend?"

Astonished, Carol gaped at him. "What?"

He gave her a closed smile. "The weekend," he said. "There's got to be something to do around here — I don't mean in Quantico. Just the two of us. Maybe we could go up to Washington. Sample the nightlife."

"Thanks, but I don't think so."

His smile disappeared. "I was thinking we could have some fun together."

Close to showing her amusement at the very thought, Carol said demurely, "It's kind of you to think of me, but no thank you."

Yench narrowed his eyes and, without speaking again, turned away.

Going back for a second mug of coffee, Carol saw Debra Caulfield and Ian Forteys deep in conversation. The Scotsman's face was flushed, and he had one hand on Debra's arm in an almost proprietary gesture. Carol caught a snatch of conversation. As she passed them, Ian hissed, "I'll get the bastard!"

Debra said quickly, "No, don't do anything. You'll only make it worse."

Bearing in mind Leota's request to pick up anything she could, Carol lingered near the couple, hoping to get more, but Nikki Lee, bubbling with her usual good humor, claimed Carol's attention.

"Carol," she said in her incongruous English accent, coming as it did from an Asian face, "if you've read your class schedule, you know we're having instruction in nonlethal weapons tomorrow, and one has to have a partner. I choose you." She cocked her head. "Well? Aren't you honored?"

It was impossible not to like Nikki. Carol smiled as she said, "I am honored. Deeply, in fact."

"Good. I thought I'd save you from Mike Yench. I'm sure he'd team up with you if he had the chance." Her dark eyes were inquisitive. "I hope you wanted to be saved."

"I don't need saving, but thanks anyway."

She looked at Nikki thoughtfully, thinking that it would be easy to underestimate her. Carol wondered if underneath that cheerful manner there might not be someone a great deal more formidable.

After the final session of the day, Carol put on her quilted jacket and walked over to the library, which was administered, her orientation folder told her in impeccable FBI-speak, by the Office of Information and Learning Resource. It was a square, squat, unadorned building with external concrete pillars encasing glass walls.

Carol knew it was possibly one of the most comprehensive law enforcement libraries in the world, where, in addition to on-line resources, the audiovisual materials, legal publications, government documents, and periodicals were constantly updated.

Inside the library's welcome warm silence, she found the most recent information on ecstasy without trouble. Carol was familiar with the drug in Australia, but now she was more interested in its manufacture and distribution in Britain and America.

Ecstasy had first been synthesized in 1912, but had been ignored until the seventies, when it was used in therapy sessions. Its use had been legal in the States until the mid-eighties, when the DEA banned the substance because some studies showed it might cause brain damage.

At first a club drug restricted to a small elite, the use of ecstasy, or *e*, had exploded into a much wider community and had become wildly popular, particularly with the young. It was related to both amphetamines and mescaline; Carol blinked at the drug's chemical name: methylene dioxymethamphetamine. This was generally shortened, mercifully, to MDMA.

Called the "hug drug" by many because users expressed feelings of euphoria and empathy for others, it was, Carol realized, an almost perfect substance to market. E was cheap and easy to make, was distributed in pill form — manufacturers even used individual colors, shapes, and imprints to identify their pills — and required no needles or other apparatus. And, unlike heroin and cocaine, ecstasy had a reputation for being harmless and fun, although it was often cut with other substances that might have adverse side effects.

One of the largest production areas for MDMA was a rural area near the Dutch-Belgian border, not far from Brussels airport. Organized crime, drawn by the huge profits, had moved in and set up worldwide distribution networks. Checking the seizure figures, Carol found that e was obviously pouring into both Britain and the United States at an ever-accelerating rate.

Carol sat back and considered what she'd learned. If Sir Richard Rackham had been involved in the ecstasy trade, then he would have been dealing with a great deal of money. An American study showed that a single pill costing around ten cents to manufacture could be sold for thirty dollars on the streets of New York. A hundred pounds of ecstasy could fetch thirty million dollars. The figures for ecstasy pills flooding into London were comparable.

Leota had told Carol that a Scotland Yard

undercover police investigation, code-named Operation Soda, had been gathering incriminating evidence against Rackham, and his arrest had been put on hold while further information about his co-conspirators was gathered. Carol had asked if Debra Caulfield or Mike Yench had been implicated, and was told that so far there were only suspicions, but no hard facts.

Carol pushed back her chair. The huge sums of money generated by illegal drugs attracted organized crime, and violence was an everyday commodity. Perhaps Sir Richard Rackham was dead. Or perhaps he'd felt the breath of his pursuers on his neck, and morphed into a new identity somewhere safe, like Brazil, which had no extradition treaties.

She gazed out the window at the trees whipping in a wind she knew would cut like a razor. If Rackham were in Brazil, at least he would be warm.

For part of the way back to the dormitory building Carol was protected by a covered walkway, but then she had to brave the darkening air. Hands shoved in pockets and cursing because she'd forgotten her gloves, she was nearly to the dormitory building when she felt her heart jump as someone materialized beside her.

"Can we talk?" said Debra Caulfield.

Carol nodded. "Inside, though. It's damn cold out here."

They found a quiet corner in a downstairs

sitting room where a television set, volume turned down, danced its images to empty seats. Carol shrugged off her jacket and settled into an armchair. "What's up?" she said.

Debra looked at her for a long moment. "I saw you with Leota Woolfe. I want to know what she said to you about me . . . and Mike."

"We discussed Sir Richard Rackham." Carol watched for a reaction, but Debra's bleak expression didn't change. Carol leaned forward. "Why did you leave the polygraph session this morning?"

A small smile tugged at Debra's mouth. "Leave?" she said in her precise British accent. "I rather thought I stormed out."

"Well, that too," said Carol. "You really irritated Agent Vertelle, which can only be a good thing."

Debra did smile at that. "He is a tiresome little man." She sobered to add, "I'm being set up for a fall. That's what was happening this morning."

Carol leaned back, surveying Debra thoughtfully. "Sir Richard appears to have been dealing in illegal substances," she said. "Are you involved?"

Debra shook her head. "You're direct. I'll give you that."

"Can I have a direct answer?"

"We were on the case — me and Mike Yench. Ecstasy was coming into England from the

Continent, huge shipments that were funneled through a new network. When we started to get whispers that Sir Richard was implicated, I didn't believe it, thought it was a smear meant to damage him politically."

"What changed your mind?"

Debra spread her hands. "You know how it is — there were too many inconsistencies, too many leads that pointed in his direction. I went to Mike Yench and told him I thought Rackham was bent, that he was getting fat on the drug trade while publicly attacking it." She paused, looking down at her fingers.

"What happened?" Carol prompted.

"He's my superior." She lifted her shoulders. "He told me to keep quiet, that it was all under control, that there was an international angle and that the FBI and the DEA were involved."

"And?"

Debra gave a derisive laugh. "I obediently kept quiet, fool that I was. Now, it seems, I'm suspected of being involved with Rackham, and of tipping him off that Scotland Yard was closing in on him."

Carol frowned at her. "But Inspector Yench —"

"Oh yes," Debra broke in. "Mike says he supports me, that he knows it isn't true, but I'm starting to think he's willing to leave me twisting in the wind, taking the blame while he gets off scot-free."

door. She was shivering, not so much from cold, but from the adrenaline that had flooded her veins. She looked back over her shoulder, half expecting Mike Yench to be limping up behind her, but there was no sign of him. Getting at the end of a line for food, she took a deep breath to calm herself and looked around. Light conversation wasn't something she wanted to endure at the moment, so she didn't want to sit with anyone she knew.

"You okay?" asked Ian Forteys, joining the queue.

She turned to face him. "I'm fine."

"You look a bit stressed." He grinned. "It must be all that learning we're doing, eh?"

Looking over his shoulder at the doorway, she said, "Must be." She didn't think Mike Yench would cause a scene in front of everyone in the dining hall, but he was drunk, so it was a possibility.

Ian Forteys followed her glance. "Waiting for someone?"

She changed her focus to him. "You've got a lot of questions tonight, Ian."

"Two," he said. "That's all I've asked, but since you mention it, I do have another. How much influence do you have with Leota Woolfe?"

"Influence? None."

"Oh, come on, Carol, I saw you two talking together. It's obvious you know her well."

"I've met her a couple of times. That's all."

He brushed off her words with an abrupt gesture. "Has Debra spoken to you? She said she was going to." When Carol nodded, he went on, "She's being set up, I know it. She'll take the fall, and Yench will come out pure as snow."

Raising an eyebrow, Carol said, "This is quite a conversion for you, isn't it? Yesterday you were telling me the two of them were crooks. Today he's the villain and she's the innocent victim. Why the change?"

"I've talked to Debra."

"She must be very persuasive."

A flash of anger flickered on Forteys's pale face. "She and Yench were sent here to the Academy, they didn't volunteer for this course. Did you know that?"

"Debra mentioned it last night."

Balancing a laden tray, Nikki stopped beside them. "Hey, you two, we've commandeered a table over in the corner." She jerked her head toward Debra, Lars, Karfer, and the lone New Zealander in the class — a softly spoken man with a wrestler's build. "See you there."

Looking after her, Forteys said to Carol, "Nikki Lee's in tight with the feds. She went undercover in Hong Kong to get the goods on Chinese triads setting up in California. She's ruthless — would turn her own mother in if it meant Nikki got kudos." He tapped the side of his nose. "A word to the wise — don't tell Nikki anything you don't want the FBI to know."

"I don't have any secrets," said Carol.

"That's not what I've heard," he said with a tight smile.

With a pulse of irritation, Carol said, "You seem to hear a lot, Ian."

"It goes with being a cop." His flippant tone evaporated as he went on, "About Debra — I'd appreciate it if you can find out anything, anything at all. She can't rely on a word Yench says because he's getting ready to throw her to the wolves. She's tried calling friends at Scotland Yard, but got nowhere."

"I'll do what I can." As she said this, Carol realized that she wasn't just saying this to placate Ian Forteys but that she actually meant it. Debra Caulfield had been convincing when Carol had talked with her, and Carol felt a growing respect for her. Maybe, Carol had to admit, her opinion was influenced by the fact that Mike Yench was a brute. But it seemed a real possibility that Debra was being set up by Yench to divert attention from, at best, his shortcomings, and at worst, his criminal behavior.

CHAPTER EIGHT

Mike Yench didn't turn up at dinner, and Carol, though she kept a wary eye out, didn't see him again that night. She wondered if anyone had seen the skirmish, or if Yench had told anyone about it. Certainly there were no comments that indicated any class member knew what had happened.

Without the slightest twinge of guilt, she considered whether the kick might have smashed his patella. If so, he would need medical attention. Perhaps he'd collapsed where she'd left him. She visualized the scene: He'd been hunched over, his face a mask of rage. No, she was sure he was able to walk, although, she hoped, with considerable discomfort.

The group were to have several days of instruction on new developments in lethal and nonlethal weapons, and Vertelle had scheduled a short introductory video for them to see that evening. Carol got there early and watched the others straggle in, clearly unenthusiastic, except for Nikki, who was her buoyant self, and Karfer, who fancied himself an expert on crowd control and was happy to tell anyone who'd listen about the latest methods to immobilize rioters.

"Foam from a glue gun," he was saying. "Sounds too stupid to be true, but it works. The crims get stuck in it, can't walk, can't move, and everything they touch gets glued to them. Laugh a minute."

Carol saw Debra come in, followed a few minutes later by Ian Forteys, looking gray faced. She noticed they didn't sit together and was going to move over to the vacant seat next to Debra's when a chunky woman she'd never seen before took it and began a conversation with Debra.

"Are we all here?" Agent Vertelle's nasal voice asked. He checked off their names, clicking his tongue with annoyance when three of the twelve were absent. "Sukani, Harris, and Yench — where are they?"

"Sukani has got a call in to the Philippines," someone volunteered. "He'll be here as soon as possible."

"You're late, Harris," Vertelle snapped as the Canadian appeared at the door. "Now, where's Yench?"

When no one offered a reply, he slapped his folder down on the lectern. "We'll begin without him."

Carol half watched the screen as a series of new nonlethal weapons were shown. The first devices included pepper balls, which were fired from a distance to shatter in blinding droplets, a similar product that produced a smell so foul that it was incapacitating, and the gluey foam that Karfer had been talking about, which left subjects covered in a sticky substance that made movement impossible.

These products were followed by much more disturbing weapons, many developed by the Pentagon for military applications but now under review for use in law enforcement generally. These included acoustic devices that generated sonic waves to cause dizziness and nausea, vortex weapons that fired invisible doughnut-shaped shock waves, and microwave guns that disturbed brain and heart function. Each of these, at sufficient intensity, could kill.

"More creative than bullets," said Nikki Lee approvingly, leaning forward from the seat behind Carol as the video ended. "I can think of several worthy victims when we try those weapons out on the range tomorrow."

"Such as?"

"Mike Yench for one." Nikki's tone was scathing. "He propositioned me, would you believe that? Coarse, hulking boor that he is. I told him where to get off."

Carol twisted around in her seat to look at Nikki. "When was this?"

"Right after the last class ended." Dropping her voice to approximate Yench's deep growl, Nikki said, "I love Asian women — they're special." Back in her normal tone she added, "What a cretin."

"It's a blow," said Carol sardonically, "to find myself second choice. Mike Yench put the hard word on me shortly before dinner."

"Hard word?" said Nikki. "Sounds painful."

"It was for him."

When Carol recounted what had happened, Nikki spluttered with laughter. "I'd have loved to have seen that!"

"You beating up on men again, Carol?" Peter Karfer had an edge in his voice, although he was smiling.

Nikki punched his arm. "Only those who deserve it. Have you seen Mike Yench anywhere? He'll be limping, when you do."

"People?" Agent Vertelle's voice cut sharply into the buzz of conversation in the room. He tapped the lectern several times, and the noise level dropped. "I'd like to introduce Agent Nancy Pyke. She will be assisting us on the range tomorrow."

The square woman who'd been sitting beside Debra had joined Vertelle. She surveyed the room with a basiliscine stare. "Good evening," she snapped.

"I don't like the look of her," said Karfer.

"Looks can be deceiving," said Nikki. "Take you as an example, Pete. You look quite nice."

Leota met Carol as she left the room. "Buy you a coffee?"

"Sure."

As they strolled alone across the open ground between buildings, taking a shortcut from the pathway, Carol was wondering whether to tell Leota about her self-defense effort with Yench. Deciding against it, but not quite sure why, she said casually, "It's not as cold tonight."

Looking up at the starlit sky, Leota said, "It will be later — there's no cloud cover." A few steps farther on, she put her hand on Carol's shoulder. "Cold weather's good for snuggling."

Carol turned her head to look into Leota's face, thinking how her dark skin emphasized the whiteness of her teeth. Carol found herself wondering what it would be like to kiss that smiling mouth. Carol said, "Are you coming on to me?"

"Of course. Is that a problem?"

"I'm not sure. Perhaps it is."

Dropping her hand from Carol's shoulder, Leota said, "I can't see why, unless you're deeply involved with someone else, and you aren't, are you?"

"That's sounds as if you've been researching me."

"If I have, it's because I didn't want to embarrass myself by having you reject me out of hand." Leota chuckled, the sound a warm caress in the dark air. "That is, if you should be so foolish."

They walked a few more steps in silence, then Leota said, "What do you say?"

"I'm thinking about it."

Leota stepped into the scant cover provided by a clump of evergreen shrubs. "Come here, and I'll give you something to help you make up your mind."

Grinning, Carol joined her. "You'll be asking me to hop into the backseat of your car next."

"That's my next move, if this doesn't work."

What the hell, Carol thought. *Why not?*

They were almost the same height. Leota unzipped Carol's jacket and slid her hands underneath it to wrap her arms around Carol. "Ready?"

Carol said, "This had better be worth it."

"It will be, but you can rate me if you like," murmured Leota against Carol's mouth.

The first kiss, thought Carol, *how many have there been in my life*? A sudden reluctance made her pull away, but Leota didn't release her. "Carol," she said, "don't tease me."

It was unexpected — the sweetness of this slow, thorough kiss. Carol was ready to welcome uncomplicated passion, with no strings attached, but there was no hint of urgency in Leota, no hint of reckless, driving passion.

Carol felt a gradual heat suffuse her, spreading through her like honey in her veins. And then a throb of hard desire. "Hey," she said, drawing back from Leota's mouth, "slow and easy certainly does it."

Leota nuzzled Carol's neck. "I always take my time," she breathed. "And the longer I take, the better it is."

Tingling, Carol said, "I can believe it."

A burst of conversation and laughter came from the pathway nearby. Leota released Carol and stood back.

"I've spoken to Hal and Jill, and when they told me they'd asked you to spend next weekend with them in Washington, I said I'd drive you up." In the darkness, Carol couldn't make out her expression, but her voice was warm. "It's three days away. A long time."

Carol felt a warm tendril of desire curling inside her. "I can wait," she said.

CHAPTER NINE

If the weather had been like the day before, Carol would have gone for her run inside the gymnasium complex, but the morning dawned cold and clear, with a cloudless sky and the promise of bright sunshine. She checked the lacing of her shoes, did a few cursory stretches — she was always aware she skimped on these —

and began a slow jog in the direction of Hogan's Alley.

As she ran, she thought about Leota Woolfe. Carol wanted to believe that it was just a case of simple attraction between them, but she couldn't dismiss the nagging feeling that the FBI agent might have some hidden agenda. Her caution was put to one side as she contemplated the coming weekend in Washington. She had a sudden delicious sense of liberation. Being in another country, where she was a stranger, brought with it a freedom to act without worrying about the pattern of relationships — both work and personal — that delineated her life in Sydney.

She reached Hogan's Alley and ran down the mock city street. Behind the facades replicating the town were classrooms, storage areas, and maintenance offices. She swung past the track used for pursuit-and-defensive-driving training, and turned back toward the main buildings.

Carol's breath came easily, and the sound of her steps was a steady metronome. She felt alive, exhilarated. Sydney seemed very far away, as though it were another life altogether, where she had left behind the cares, the worries, and the quandaries of her usual existence.

Approaching the main complex from a different direction to the way she'd set out, Carol came upon a small knot of people gathered around something on the ground at the edge of a stand of trees near the dormitory buildings. There was something about the way they were standing that brought a chill of certainty. She knew, with an instinct beyond logic, that someone had died.

She slowed to a walk. The group parted as she came up to them, and she could see a body lying facedown, one arm curled protectively around its head. A heavy stainless-steel wristwatch caught the thin morning sun.

Carol looked at the bristle of short red hair on the scalp, the slumped, heavy form. Although she could only see part of the face, she said without hesitation, "It's Mike Yench. What happened?"

A maintenance man in overalls and a fleece-lined red jacket frowned at her. "Been dead for hours," he said. "Stiff as a board." He pointed to the congealed blood that had run from a wound above the right eye. "I'd say that's what killed him." The blood looped down his exposed cheek and disappeared under his chin. Another dark trickle came from Yench's ear.

Someone murmured behind her as Carol stared down at the body, then at the man who had spoken to her, seeing every detail of his face with strange clarity. He'd shaved carelessly, and there was a patch of gray stubble at the angle of his jaw. "This area will have to be cordoned off," she said with authority. "Everyone should move away, to avoid contaminating the scene further."

Without complaint, they obeyed her instruction. Carol looked at the ground. There were no footprints, and the surface seemed undisturbed around the body. Her eyes were drawn back to Yench. In her career, she'd seen many dead bodies and experience had hardened her, but this time was different. She realized with a shock that unless it was an accidental death, she herself could be one of several suspects.

Disbelief flooded through her. How often had she observed a death scene with a feeling of professional anticipation, feeling the pleasure of meeting a challenge, the satisfaction of being one of the agents of justice? But here, out of her familiar world, she had no authority. She wouldn't be asking the questions — she'd be answering them.

After breakfast Vertelle called the class to order, quieting the agitated hum that had greeted him. His glance flickering from person to person as he spoke, saying without ceremony, "As most of you seem to know already, Chief Inspector Michael Yench was found dead this morning." Vertelle's angular features showed extreme displeasure, as though this was not what he expected from a participant in a course for which he was responsible.

Carol had a moment's cold amusement that it took death to make Agent Vertelle use a class member's full name and rank.

"What happened? Who found him?" Nikki

Lee's voice was flat, her usual exuberance dampened.

"There will be an autopsy, of course," said Vertelle, biting off the words with cold precision, "but it seems that he fell heavily, striking his head, and sustaining a fatal wound. His body was found by a groundskeeper this morning, but it appears the incident may have occurred some time last evening."

"An accident?" said Ian Forteys. Carol saw him glance over at Debra on the other side of the room. "Yench had been drinking; I smelled it on his breath."

Vertelle drew the corners of his mouth down in a grimace. "I'm surprised you seem unaware that the first rule of detection is never to leap to conclusions, Forteys."

Red staining his pale cheeks, Forteys said harshly, "So now you're saying it could be murder, are you?"

Debra put a hand to her mouth. Carol heard someone behind her take a deep breath. Her own thoughts tumbled possibilities in her head. Murder was always a case of who, how, and when. And *why* was often the key that unlocked the mystery. Why would someone want Mike Yench dead?

A new idea swam to the surface — what if it had been a hit? Yench was involved in some way in a billion-dollar illegal industry, a multinational activity with webs of influence transcending national boundaries. Was it so outlandish to imagine that his death had been planned as a business decision, possibly somewhere outside the United States?

Of course, Carol chided herself, all this was interesting to consider, but it was pure supposition, and the scenario that Mike Yench had died in a drunken fall was far more likely.

She became aware of Vertelle's abrasive voice. He was saying, ". . . investigation will be held, and each of you can expect to be questioned in due course." He tapped the bottom of his folder on the lectern in the manner of one who has completed an unpleasant duty. "Practical demonstration of nonlethal weapons will begin at ten sharp. I expect you to be on the range, fully equipped, by that time."

Carol scanned the faces of her classmates. Debra Caulfield looked remote, almost bored, as though she'd had no connection to Yench, as though his demise was a matter of little interest to her. In contrast, Peter Karfer was animated, chatting to Sukani and Harris. Ian Forteys, his face somber, sat by himself, watching Debra Caulfield.

Curious, Carol went over to him. "Ian? What do you think?"

Her mild question elicited a strong response. "I'm glad the bastard's dead," he said loudly, his Scottish brogue very noticeable. "And gone, I hope, to his well-deserved place in hell."

Hearing his vehement words, several people turned to look at him. Carol said, "It may not be wise to say things like that until we know it was an accident."

"Of course it was an accident." Debra's voice was as cool as her face. "Mike was falling-down drunk last night." Distaste twisted her mouth. "Mike's luggage had more bottles of Scotch than clothes."

"I never thought of Magic Mike as a boozer," said Karfer, a note of accusation in his voice. "All the time I was in London, I never saw Mike get really pissed. Not once."

Debra made a contemptuous sound. "You'd be an expert on this, would you, Pete?"

Nettled, he said, "I bloody would, Deb. Why are you trying to make Mike out as a drunk when he wasn't?" His smile was dangerous. "It almost seems like you're trying to make it sound more likely that he fell over and killed himself, rather than that someone did him in."

Shortly after ten Carol was on the firing range feeling self-conscious in an outfit that included a flak jacket and protective apron, a helmet, shatterproof goggles, and heavy earmuffs to preserve her hearing. Similarly attired, Nikki faced her, hefting a heavy-barreled vortex cannon. To either side of them others in the class were ranged in couples. With Mike Yench gone, they were an odd number, and the place was taken by Agent Vertelle, who was partnering Debra Caulfield. Looking at Vertelle, Carol hoped she didn't look as comical as he did in his outfit.

"Ready? Prepare to fire at my signal." Agent Nancy Pyke's voice, even using a bullhorn, was distant and fuzzy through the ear protection.

Carol squinted at Nikki, who was grinning beneath her goggles, her enthusiasm again at full strength. She'd whooped when Carol lost the toss, so becoming the passive victim. Nancy Pyke had made it clear that there was no danger but possibly some discomfort. The vortex cannons were at the lowest setting so they'd deliver a mild shock wave of much less intensity than that used in confrontational situations.

Looking down the fat barrel of the portable cannon Nikki had pointed at her chest, Carol wondered what would happen if someone, with malice or by mistake, upped the intensity to full strength. The demonstration they had seen on the video indicated that death was a possibility.

"Fire!" came faintly through her ear protection, then Carol staggered back as the spinning vortex ring, completely invisible, smacked into her. It was similar to the effect of being slapped by a huge flat paddle.

Nikki's keenness waned markedly when it was

her turn to be the subject, but by lunchtime both she and Carol were old hands at the game. With Agent Pyke superintending, they and the other members of the class had set up acoustic barriers, which were actually sonic speakers broadcasting frequencies that caused anyone in range to experience sensations akin to motion sickness, complete with dizziness and nausea. They had also fired dummy pepper balls and riot-control rubber pellets at each other and had used a small personal weapon the size of a pack of cigarettes that caused complete paralysis for several minutes by scrambling signals from the brain to voluntary muscles.

When Carol was the victim of this harmless-looking device, she felt as if a million sharp points were speeding through her body. Her breathing and other vital functions were unaffected, but, although conscious, she couldn't move. Lying there, a wave of panic broke over her. What if the paralysis didn't fade away? Then, with a wash of relief, she found she could move again. She rolled over and got to her feet. "I never want to go through that again."

Nikki, who'd experienced its effects first, made a face at her. "Don't be a wimp, Carol."

"I'm trying to be as brave as you, Nikki, but it's hard."

"Now you're being sarcastic," said Nikki. She

held up the little box. "You know, size is irrelevant. You could bring down the biggest guy on earth before he knew what was happening."

"A perfect woman's weapon?"

Nikki laughed. "Equalize things a bit, wouldn't it?"

Carol wondered if Nikki had had the same thought — Mike Yench, hefty though he was, could have been immobilized with something like this and then killed. She mentally shook her head. For her own sake, she didn't want his death to be anything but an accident, although she couldn't deny her growing certainty that Mike Yench's death was murder.

Walking back with Nikki to the dining hall for lunch, Carol took the opportunity to follow up the comment Ian Forteys had made last night. "Have you had much to do with the FBI in your job?" she asked in a conversational tone.

Nikki looked sideways at her. "And who's been talking to you?"

Keeping it light, Carol shot her an amused glance. "Is this paranoia I hear in your voice, Nikki?"

"Quite possibly. This wouldn't have come from Forteys, would it?"

Hiding her surprise at Nikki's accuracy, Carol said, "Why would you say that?"

"He's an odd guy, so watch out for him. Forteys is the type who bears grudges and who never forgets a slight. You heard what he said about Yench this morning. That all goes back to the fact that Forteys had a girlfriend who chose to work with Yench rather than to go back to Edinburgh with him."

"You mean Debra?"

Nikki nodded. "You notice how he's following her around? Creepy guy." She looked keenly at Carol. "It *was* him, wasn't it? What did he say about me?"

Carol debated whether to evade the question, then decided to be direct. "Ian told me you'd been working with the FBI undercover in Hong Kong. And that you'd remained, as he put it, tight with the feds."

"All true," said Nikki. "Is that all?"

"And that you were ruthless."

Nikki chuckled. "Also true."

Wondering how Nikki knew so much about Forteys, Yench, and Debra Caulfield, Carol said, "You've obviously run into these British cops before. Was it through the FBI?"

"You hear how I talk, like a proper English lady?" she said sardonically. "Ever wondered why?"

"I'd guess that you went to school in England."

"Very good," Nikki acknowledged. "Hong Kong was still an English colony, and my family were well off, and could afford to have me educated in the United Kingdom. And then, later, I did my police training in London. That's where I met Debra."

"I didn't realize that, before this course, you were friends."

"We're not," said Nikki. "We know each other, that's all."

The interviews were conducted during the afternoon. Carol's came late, after most in the class had been done. Vertelle had loudly complained that he'd had to reschedule the course to take into account these unscheduled absences, and by the time the call came for Carol he was in a thoroughly bad mood. "Make it snappy, Ashton," he said. "Just keep to the point and don't bother giving the long version."

Carol, who was angry with herself because she was unaccountably nervous about the whole thing, snapped back, "I consider that an unprofessional request."

Vertelle's face darkened, but Carol exited before he could come back with a reply.

The interviews were held in a small office in one of the administrative buildings. Carol followed the junior FBI agent who'd been sent to escort her, thinking wryly that once the detectives heard her story, it wouldn't surprise her if they immediately wheeled in a lie detector to test her truthfulness.

The principal interviewer was a detective with the Virginia police, who was assisted by two FBI agents Carol had never seen before. There was no polygraph, but the proceedings were both video-taped and audiotaped, and one wall of the room was a two-way mirror. Carol glanced at her own reflection, wondering if observers were concealed behind it.

It was unnerving to be the interviewee and not the interviewer, and Carol was annoyed to find herself concerned about how she looked and how she sounded. She freely described the alter-cation she and Mike Yench had had and why she had been compelled to use physical force to get away from him. Listening to herself speak, she worried if it sounded too rehearsed.

Carol expected that the admission that she'd tried to incapacitate Yench would generate many probing questions, especially if Nikki Lee had already told them about the incident, but the interviewer, a pleasant-looking man who had in-troduced himself as Detective James Lewis, didn't appear to be particularly impressed. He only asked for clarification on exactly where and when this had happened, and if Yench had sustained any blows to his head during the incident.

Lewis seemed more interested in how she had come upon the body the next morning. He listened to her explanation, then asked a series of questions about where she'd run and why she'd come back to the building by that particular route.

The FBI agents assisting him asked for clarification on a couple of points, and then she was thanked, advised that there might be further questions later, and let go.

It wasn't the way Carol would have run the questioning had she been in charge, and she was puzzling about it as she started back to the class. She'd been treated far too leniently, she thought, considering that she'd had a physical confrontation with the victim the night of his death.

"How's it feel being interrogated as a hapless subject?" asked Leota, catching up to Carol as she was about to step out into the sunshine.

Surprised, Carol turned to face her. "Have you been lurking around waiting for me to pass by?"

"Certainly I have. How did it go?"

Carol raised her shoulders. "Piece of cake. I thought I was going to be grilled, but they just let me tell my story. They asked a few questions, and that was that." She gave Leota a small smile. "Quite disappointing, really."

"It pays to have friends in high places."

"What do you mean?"

"I mean, my dear Carol, that I made it clear that Detective Inspector Ashton would never lie."

Looking at her narrowly, Carol said, "You were on the other side of the mirror."

Not the slightest quelled by Carol's combative tone, Leota said, "Guilty as charged."

"I'm astonished that you aren't demanding why I didn't tell you about the fight I had with Yench." Before Leota could answer, Carol went on, "But you knew already, didn't you? I imagine Nikki Lee told you all about it."

Leota nodded. "Excellent deduction. It's fortunate she did; otherwise, I wouldn't have known I had to go to bat for you."

Affronted that Leota had assumed that she couldn't cope on her own, Carol said, "I'm not so sure I needed you."

"You did, believe me."

Her calm assurance vexed Carol. "I've got to get back to class," she said, to end the conversation.

"I'll walk you back." After a few steps she chuckled. "Don't frown, Carol. If it makes you feel better, you probably didn't need my help. I watched the whole interview, and you were very good. Of course, blond and beautiful always helps."

"I love to be stereotyped."

Leota reacted to Carol's exasperation by adding mockingly, "And intelligent and cool. Did I forget to say that?"

"Fine," said Carol, "but if the postmortem shows he was murdered, then they'll be back to get me, quick smart."

"The autopsy is tomorrow," said Leota, now

serious, "but I can tell you it already looks like an accident. There's a smear of blood on the wall of the building near where he was found, and traces of blood on the ground. Several people, including you, saw him drunk, and I've got no trouble at all with a scenario that has him falling hard against the wall, stumbling a few feet, then falling down to die of brain hemorrhage and exposure during the night."

"What if it's murder?"

"If it's murder," said Leota, "we'll have suspects coming out of our ears."

CHAPTER TEN

The two days before the weekend were uncomfortably tense. Everyone seemed to find it difficult to regain the spirit of camaraderie, and the evidence tape cordoning off the area where Yench had died was a constant reminder of what had happened.

Carol didn't see Leota after Thursday afternoon, although she'd looked for her, intending to follow up on the request Ian Forteys had made to find out more about the case against Debra Caulfield.

Friday had been spent on the range with Agent Pyke giving instruction on the capabilities of new lethal weapons. The agent was a stern taskmaster, and never hesitated to correct a safety violation or a clumsy action with loud and specific criticism. The worst of her ire was directed toward Peter Karfer and the Filipino, Sukani, neither of whom could satisfy her, no matter how hard they tried.

Carol escaped unscathed as she was an excellent shot and had an aptitude for picking up the intricacies of new equipment. She usually enjoyed target practice, but a whole day of loud noises and the smell of gun oil and gunpowder gave her a headache, so she was relieved when the session was over.

Nancy Pyke directed them to return to the classroom for a debriefing. She launched into a review of the weapons they had used during the day, made a few stinging remarks about certain participants' shortcomings, directing her ire toward Forteys for a safety violation she had detected, and then turned the lectern over to Vertelle.

He pursed his thin lips until there was absolute silence in the room. Then he said in sour tones, "I am to advise you that, although inquiries are continuing, Inspector Yench's death does appear to be accidental. While intoxicated he apparently fell against a wall and sustained a serious head injury. It appears he then, semi-conscious, made his way into the cover of adjacent vegetation, where he collapsed. He lay there undiscovered until the next morning, by which time it was too late."

He paused, his gaze darting around the room, as though waiting for some response. When no one said anything, he gave a quick nod. "That's it, then."

As everyone got up to leave, Carol looked at the faces around her. If anyone felt sorry that Mike Yench was dead, the grief was well hidden. Debra Caulfield, who had been his colleague for several years, was her usual contained self. Ian Forteys, who might be expected to be content that the man he so intensely disliked was gone forever, had a dissatisfied, sullen expression. Nikki Lee was giggling over something Peter Karfer had said to her. The other members of the class appeared indifferent, although Harris, the soft-spoken Canadian, said to Carol as they trooped out of the room, "It's grim, isn't it? You can be here one day, and gone the next." He snapped his fingers. "Just like that."

Intending to shower to get the smell of dust and gunpowder out of her hair, Carol went straight back to the dormitories. She found a sealed envelope on her bed. As she picked it up,

Debra Caulfield came in. "A secret admirer, Carol?"

"I should be so lucky."

Since Yench's body had been found, Debra had been even more taciturn than usual, so Carol was pleased that she now seemed willing to indulge in light conversation. "What are you doing for the weekend?" she asked.

"I'll do the tourist bit," Debra said. "Nancy Pyke has volunteered to drive me around."

Carol stared at her, incredulous. "You mean Agent Pyke, our extraordinary firearms instructor?" Belatedly she remembered Nancy Pyke sitting beside Debra on Wednesday evening at the video showing. "I'm sorry, you obviously know her."

"I don't, actually. She was friendly the other night at the video — chatted to me about London, which apparently she loves. She's a real Anglophile, and she offered to show me around Washington if I did the same for her in London some time."

It was difficult for Carol to imagine Nancy Pyke chatting about anything, but she wasn't going to say so. "It's great if you have someone who knows the area as a guide," she said lightly.

Debra's smile was deeply cynical. "I'm not taking Nancy Pyke's offer at face value," she said. "I think it's much more likely she's been assigned to keep an eye on me, but even if that's true, I'm willing to go along with it just to get out of this place." She threw up her hands. "And especially to get away from Ian."

"I know you were friends once," said Carol ingenuously, "and I thought you'd patched things up when Ian came to me and asked if I'd intercede on your behalf with Agent Woolfe."

With a look of disgust, Debra said, "He fancies he has a chance with me again, but he's a psycho, Carol. There's something awfully wrong with him."

"Nikki Lee thinks so too."

Debra looked at her sharply. "She's a plant."

"Is she?"

"Ask Leota Woolfe. She knows all about it." Debra snatched up her towel. "I'm going to have a shower."

As soon as she had gone, Carol opened the envelope. Leota's writing was small and neat. *Pick you up at ten tomorrow. It takes about forty-five minutes from the Academy to Washington. Not long enough, Carol. But save Saturday night for me. All night. I don't intend to be hurried.*

Carol smiled at the signature, *Your Agent.*

Saturday morning was clear and sunny, with a hint of spring in the air and the promise that, at least in the middle of the day, the temperature might climb into a range Carol would consider comfortable. Carol packed an overnight bag, lingering over what to take for dinner that night, as Hal had said he had a booking at one of the best restaurants in the capital.

Leota was punctual, and soon after ten they were on the I-95 freeway and on the way to Washington. Carol didn't feel like talking, but rather just enjoying the liberty from not only the demands of the course, but also from the strange, disordered atmosphere that had followed Mike Yench's death.

Leota filled the silence with details of the autopsy and the investigation so far. "If it's murder, it's an efficient one," she said. "The blood on the wall is Yench's; the wound itself has microscopic traces that match the building material. The blood alcohol was high enough to make him very drunk." She grinned at Carol. "And apart from a hairline crack of the skull, he had a chipped patella and badly bruised knee, plus an abrasion on his shin."

Carol didn't smile back, as she'd been haunted by the disturbing thought that maybe Yench had stumbled into the wall because she'd hurt his knee so badly, and she was partly responsible for what had happened next, as, dazed, Yench had staggered out of view of anyone passing by, and had lain unconscious in the bitter cold, his brain hemorrhaging until he died from the pressure in his head.

"You're not still brooding over Yench, are you?" said Leota, accelerating into the fast lane.

"I was thinking about him, yes."

Leota gave a short, unamused laugh. "He wasn't worth it when he was alive, and he's certainly not worth it now."

Carol studied Leota's profile. She had a strong nose and a stronger chin, and her dark skin shone with health. Carol thought of putting out a finger and stroking the line of her jaw. Instead she said, "You sound as if you disliked him personally."

"I did. The more I learned about Magic Mike Yench the more I despised him."

"Because he was a crooked cop?"

"More than that. He perverted others. Sergeant Debra Caulfield, for one. Everything shows she had a great future until she fell in with him."

Seizing the opportunity, Carol said, "I gather that Debra thinks she's being groomed to be the fall guy, and that little trick of yours with the lie detector was part of the program."

Leota turned her head. "Does she? It's a bit late for her to claim innocence. I believe she cooperated with Sir Richard, and now that he's out of the picture she's scrambling to protect her back. Yench's dying is a bonus for her, because now she'll work to make sure he gets all the blame, and he can't contradict her."

"Is there any possibility that she's not involved and that Yench, and perhaps others, have made it look bad for her?"

Leota tilted her head. "Anything is possible,

but I don't think so. Apart from Mike Yench, who's definitely implicated, someone was feeding inside information about the ongoing investigation to Sir Richard Rackham. She looks like the best bet to me."

"She claims that she went to Yench and told him that Rackham was involved and that he told her it was all under control and to keep quiet about it."

"My," said Leota, looking sideways at Carol, "Caulfield has been pouring her heart out to you."

"Unlike you," said Carol dryly.

"What's that mean?"

"You've never given me the full picture. In Los Angeles you give me this song and dance about FBI international liaison and how I've been chosen to fit in with that, and then when I get to Quantico, it becomes clear that it's a lot more to do with Rackham's disappearance and the international drug trade, and that I'm to be a plant like Nikki Lee."

That got a reaction, Carol was pleased to see. Leota turned her head quickly, a look of surprise on her face. "She's not a plant. She's liaised with us on other matters, so it's natural that she would help us on an informal basis if the opportunity came up."

"I feel everyone but me knows what's going on."

"I'm sorry, Carol, but you as a professional

know that it's almost always best to never let your right hand know what your left is doing."

Carol snorted at Leota's sweet-talking tone. "I don't know what any hands are doing. That's the trouble."

Leota's teeth flashed white. "So what do you want to know?"

Not wanting to let this opportunity get away from her, Carol said, "For now I've got two questions, but I'll save others for later."

Laughing, Leota said, "Shoot!"

"What's your best guess about Rackham's disappearance?"

After considering the question for a moment, Leota said, "Two possibilities, and you can take your pick. First, he skipped, changed his identity, and is living the good life somewhere that he considers safe. Second, he's dead, killed by partners or competitors in the drug trade. He either went willingly or was abducted, but either way he's dead and buried where no one will find him."

"Do you favor one of the two?"

"Sure. He had plenty of time to set it up. I think he's still alive and laughing at us." She glanced at a road sign. "You'd better hurry up with your second question; we're making good time."

Carol said, "Why does Hal del Bosco need a bodyguard?"

"Money laundering."

Raising her eyebrows at this succinct reply,

Carol said, "You're telling me Hal is into money laundering?"

"No, but his client is, and that brings him close to some extremely dangerous people. Don't think of Michele Rackham as an innocent party, because she isn't. And that's why she retained Hal to represent her — she's afraid that she'll be arrested."

"Then why stay here?" Carol asked. "Why not go back to London and, if necessary, fight extradition?"

"Because money laundering is big business in America, which makes it just the place to process hot cash, and the Rackhams have moved literally millions into this country with just that in mind. We've traced some of it to various centers where financial services specialize in legitimizing crime profits."

"This is money Sir Richard made in Britain from ecstasy?"

"Not just in Britain," said Leota with grudging admiration. "Rackham was in the process of extending his business, getting involved in an existing network that channels ecstasy into the States. That's why we became particularly interested in him."

Carol visualized Michele Rackham's tall, bony frame and strong features. "Are you saying she's acting as her husband's agent?"

Leota shot her an amused look. "Any reason why a woman can't run a successful business on her own? Maybe she's taken over the whole outfit."

Perversely wanting to defend the woman, Carol said, "Are you so sure she's involved? Have you got hard evidence?"

Leota sighed. "The Bureau doesn't make a habit of persecuting the innocent, Carol. Our government is increasing scrutiny in the main regions where money laundering and financial crime most often occurs — New York and New Jersey, Los Angeles, San Juan, Puerto Rico, and the border of Arizona and Texas. I suppose you'll say it's a coincidence that Michele Rackham has made eight visits to the States in the past two years and that she's spent some time in several of these areas."

"Circumstantial," said Carol, "unless you've got her on tape in incriminating circumstances."

Leota grunted with satisfaction. "We've got her on tape."

Money laundering was a rising problem in Australia as well as the rest of the world. Carol was familiar with the processes that moved the proceeds of criminal activity through a series of bank accounts until the money appeared to be the legitimate profits from legal businesses. Billions of dollars from Russia had been laundered by the

Bank of New York, and she'd seen estimates that put the worldwide laundering industry at over six hundred billion dollars.

Carol said, "Why haven't you arrested the Rackhams before now?"

"We had word that a huge shipment was coming into the country this month, and we were going to spring the trap. Then Rackham disappeared. We held off, waiting to see what had happened to him. And there's political pressure too, of course. The British prime minister isn't happy with the prospect of having one of his ministers arrested for drug trafficking, so he's been asking for time to take the appropriate political steps in London."

With a cynical smile, Carol observed, "Politicians are the same the world over."

"Ain't that the truth," said Leota. "Can't trust them as far as you can throw them."

Carol looked at her speculatively. *And how far can I trust you, Agent Woolfe?*

CHAPTER ELEVEN

Leota dropped Carol off at Hal and Jill's hotel, saying that she'd see them all that evening, and then zoomed off into traffic without saying what she was doing for the rest of the day, although Carol knew she had an apartment in Alexandria in Virginia, adjacent to Washington. *It's none of my business*, Carol thought, irritated with herself for being put out that Leota hadn't offered to show her where she lived.

The hotel was five-star, and the lobby exuded a marble and dark wood elegance. Carol checked in, went up to the room that Hal had reserved for her, and, after dropping off her overnight bag, rode the wood-paneled elevator up to the del Boscos' suite.

"Carol!" said Jill, embracing her as though they'd been separated for months, not days.

Hal, too, gave her a warm hug. She could smell his aftershave and a hint of liquor on his breath. Everything about him enhanced his image of confident affluence. He was wearing a dark gray business suit, clearly very expensive, a cream shirt, and a maroon tie. A heavy gold signet ring glinted on his right hand.

"What do you think?" he said, releasing her to gesture at the room. "Nice, isn't it?"

The suite was gorgeous, but Carol was drawn to the balcony. She went outside to feast her eyes on the views of the city. Burned into her imagination from popular culture were images of the White House, the Capitol, the Washington Monument. All were as familiar to her as Parliament House in Canberra or the Opera House and Harbour Bridge in Sydney.

Pointing, she said exultantly to Jill, "I recognize the Washington Monument."

"Hal has a business appointment," said Jill,

who was looking sensational in a pale green pant-
suit, "so we're left to our own devices. How about
a quick tour of the city, including the Washington
Monument? I've got my guidebook ready."

"What a great idea. I was hoping you'd suggest
it."

Back inside, Hal smiled indulgently at his wife.
"Notice anything different about my delightful
Jill?"

Jill cast him an exasperated look. "I've
lightened and restyled my hair," she said to Carol.
"Like it?"

"It's all your fault, Carol," Hal announced.
"She took one look at your sensational blond self
when you arrived in LA and immediately made an
appointment with the most expensive hairdresser
in Beverly Hills."

He looked at the slim gold watch on his wrist.
"I'm out of here. See you later this afternoon."

"No bodyguard?" said Carol.

Hal grinned at her. "Only in LA. Washington's
much safer."

"Pity we can't do the tour of the J. Edgar
Hoover FBI Building," said Jill as they waited for
the valet to bring her rental car from the hotel's
parking area. "It's only open to the public on
weekdays. I did the tour last time I was here, and

it's fun. There're all these exhibits with famous past cases and crime laboratories and all that stuff."

"I think I've got quite enough to do with the FBI as it is," said Carol. "Speaking of which, I've been meaning to ask you, how long have you known Leota Woolfe?"

"I don't know — a couple of years. She and Hal hit it off straightaway. He was defending a guy who was accused of sending a letter bomb to the Supreme Court. Got him off, too. But Leota didn't bear a grudge for losing the case, and we all became friends." Obviously curious, she added, "Why are you asking?"

Offhand, Carol said, "No particular reason."

Jill raised an eyebrow. "Oh, come on. You *always* have a reason."

To change the subject, Carol said, "Did you hear that someone died at the Academy on Wednesday night?"

"You're kidding!"

The valet arrived with the car at that point, so Jill's questions were delayed until they were underway. "What the hell happened?"

Carol gave her a brief account of Mike Yench's death and how, just hours before, she'd been forced to kick him to get away from his advances.

"Excellent," said Jill. "The guy sounds like a complete bastard."

"He was drunk, not that that's an excuse."

"No excuse at all. It's a pity he had to up and die just after you attacked him, but thank heavens they think it was an accident."

"That's the official line," said Carol, "but it might not be what they're really thinking. Leota gave me the results of the autopsy, and it seems open and shut, but I'm learning that federal agents don't always tell the absolute truth."

"I think you can rely on Leota," said Jill. "I know Hal trusts her completely."

"That's good," said Carol, wanting to be reassured and finding that she wasn't.

The capital was all that Carol had expected, and more. She was captivated by the Washington Monument, which stood in splendid isolation surrounded by parkland.

"Completed in 1884 and the world's tallest masonry structure at five hundred and fifty-five feet," said Jill, consulting her guidebook.

"What's that in meters?"

Jill made a face at her. "You know, I've forgotten the way we measure things in Australia. When I first got to the States I was thrown by pounds and ounces and Fahrenheit for temperature, but now it's second nature."

They joined a line of tourists, and after a short wait were whisked up the shaft by an elevator to a magnificent view that took in much of the District of Columbia and portions of Maryland and Virginia.

On their way to the Lincoln Memorial, Jill said, "I hope you don't mind, but Michele Rackham's joining us for dinner tonight. I told her Leota would be there too, but that didn't seem to bother Michele, even though she says the FBI is out to get her."

"I didn't know she was in Washington."

"Michele flew in last night. Frankly, I think she's nervous when she isn't near Hal. Somehow she thinks he's got some magic that will keep her from being arrested."

"Did you ever meet her husband?"

"Sir Richard? No, but Hal knows him."

Interested to hear Jill's opinion, Carol asked, "What do you think happened to Rackham?"

"I doubt it's kidnapping, since no one's asked for a ransom. Michele's convinced that he walked out of his own free will and that either he's in hiding somewhere or he's been hit by a car or he's fallen and that he's got amnesia and no one's identified him." She grinned. "Sounds a bit like the movie of the week to me."

"Has his wife said why he'd be likely to be hiding?"

Jill frowned at Carol. "She says it's his war on drugs — it's made him a lot of enemies. Personally, I get the impression that Sir Richard is involved in something a bit dicey, and if that's the case, I suppose he could have come to no good."

Carol could see the Doric columns of the Lincoln Memorial ahead. She wondered why she was asking questions about a case that had nothing to do with her. *I'm just a stickybeak*, she thought to herself with a smile.

"This is too much like work," she said to Jill. "Let's talk about something else."

Based on the design of a Greek temple, the Lincoln Memorial was a stunning marble building. Carol was surprised by the emotion of awe that moved her when she looked up at the huge statue of a seated President Lincoln gazing somberly out at the Reflecting Pool. His angular face had a nobility and kindness that she hadn't expected.

Then they went to the U.S. Capitol, joining a tour beneath the Rotunda. Carol thought it must be one of the most recognizable domes in the world. Her enthusiasm was blunted by the time she and Jill had finished traipsing through all the halls and chambers open to the public, as her feet were hurting and she craved the jolt only strong coffee could provide.

Later, energized by food and caffeine, they visited the Vietnam Memorial, and Carol found tears pricking her eyes as she looked at the wall of black granite panels inscribed with the names of more than fifty-eight thousand Americans, etched there in order of their deaths. There was an almost unbearable poignancy in the offerings left at the wall — flowers, photographs, letters. Australians had died in the same conflict, and Carol mused on the young men and women whose lives had been lost or irrevocably changed by the war.

They returned to the hotel in a solemn mood. An ashen-faced Michele Rackham was waiting for them in the lobby. "They've found Richard," she said. Her face crumpled. "He's dead."

Jill put an arm around her shoulders. "Do you want to sit down?"

"No, I have to go with them," Michele said, indicating two conservatively dressed young men who were standing silently nearby. "I couldn't find Hal, so I said I had to wait for you to get back."

"I'll come with you," said Jill. She looked at Carol. "Can you find out where we're going so you can tell Hal when he gets back? I'm not sure where he is, so I can't contact him."

Carol went over to the two FBI agents, who watched her warily as she approached. She identified herself and asked to see their credentials. They showed no surprise at her request, complying immediately. She ascertained where Michele Rackham and Jill were to be taken, then tried to extract information about Sir Richard. As she fully expected, a shutter came down at once, and she watched the four of them leave the lobby no wiser about Rackham's fate.

CHAPTER TWELVE

For a while it seemed that the planned dinner would have to be canceled. Hal arrived back at the hotel forty minutes after the others had left, came to Carol's room in obedience to the urgent message she had left, and then hurried off to his wife and Michele Rackham. There was no indication how long they would be, and Carol was wondering if she should contact Leota, when the agent herself called.

Sounding rushed, Leota said without ceremony, "Have you heard about Rackham?"

"Only that he's dead. His wife was waiting with the news when Jill and I got back to the hotel."

"As you can imagine, Carol, this has created quite some excitement. We're calling in extra agents from all over."

"So tonight's off?"

Leota gave a low laugh. "No way. You can't escape me that easily."

Carol felt a tingle of anticipation. Pushing it aside, she said, "How did Rackham die?"

"Back to business, I see." Leota sounded amused. "The body is too badly decomposed to tell without an autopsy."

"Where was he found?"

"Maryland, in a ditch. Rural area. Some kids stumbled over the body, and we're doing our best to make sure they don't become media heroes just yet, so don't say anything to anyone, Carol."

"It's going to get out."

"Of course it is," said Leota. "But the longer we can keep the media at bay the better."

Carol knew exactly what she meant. It wasn't that reporters contaminated crime scenes — they were controlled there — it was that they relentlessly pursued and questioned anyone who could remotely be associated with a high-profile case. It was also that the media tended to float theories, find stories where none existed, twist facts, or even lie to grab the jaded public's fleeting attention.

Leota promised to make the dinner date, warned she might be late, and rang off. Carol replaced the receiver and sat on the edge of the bed, musing. It seemed to her that if Richard Rackham's body was badly decomposed, then he must have died quite soon after his disappearance, as the weather had been frigid and his corpse had been in the open, where the cold might be expected to slow putrefaction.

She called room service and ordered a pot of coffee and, as an afterthought, a Chivas Regal whisky on the rocks. She imagined that Michele would be asked to identify her husband's remains. In circumstances like this, that was a particularly grisly task. And, as a possible suspect, she would be watched closely as she viewed the body.

Many times Carol had stood beside a relative or friend as she or he had looked at the face of someone who had once been a living, breathing individual, someone who was now inert flesh on a cold metal table. Carol knew from her own experience how sometimes a murderer, confronted with his or her handiwork, would make some damning admission, or even, in rare cases, make an outright confession to the crime.

Somehow, Carol couldn't see Michele Rackham doing that, even if she were guilty.

As it turned out, the dinner took place as planned, except that Michele Rackham was absent. "Poor Michele," said Jill. "It was *horrible*." She squinched up her face at Carol. "I can't understand how you can do that for a living. Those dead bodies . . ."

Hal patted her hand. "Just put it out of your mind, darling."

Jill glanced around the sumptuous restaurant, which was packed with diners in animated conversation and attended by hovering waiters. "I can hardly believe this afternoon ever happened. I mean, everything here looks so normal."

"Only normal for you," said Carol mockingly. "I'm certainly not accustomed to quite this level of luxury."

"You know what I mean," said Jill, a little embarrassed.

"The contrast can be good," said Leota. "It makes you appreciate what you've got." She gave a half-smile to Carol. "Or what you're going to get."

Leota looked vibrantly alive. She was wearing a black skirt and a heavy brocade silver shirt with an exaggerated collar that framed the elegant column of her neck. Her only jewelry was a pair of square silver earrings and a flat-link silver chain on her wrist.

Her wardrobe limited, Carol had fallen back on

her standby, a classic black dress. Jill was wearing its almost identical twin, although Carol had no doubt that Jill's black outfit had cost many times more than her own.

The food was delicious and was served with exquisite finesse, but Carol found herself sneaking looks at her watch. Once she glanced up from checking the time and caught Leota smiling at her. Carol knew her face was hot, and hoped no one would realize she was, incredibly for her, actually blushing.

By unspoken agreement, the conversation turned to safe topics. Jill had announced she was the designated driver, and would only have one glass of wine. Hal took her at her word, starting the meal with two martinis, and then ordering an extra bottle of wine midway through the meal.

Leota, who Carol noticed was also drinking sparingly, told amusing FBI stories, and Hal entertained them with an account of his meeting that day with a Washington lobbyist for the alternative medicine industry. "There's a lobbyist for absolutely everything," he declared. "I suspect there's even one for intergalactic aliens."

They got up from the table at eleven, and Hal went ahead to arrange for the valet service to bring the cars to the front of the restaurant. While they'd been dining the weather had changed, and a steady cold rain was falling.

Hal and Jill's vehicle arrived first. Leota had said she'd drive Carol back to the hotel, so Hal and Jill said their good-byes and went out to the car, leaving Carol and Leota in the shelter of the entrance.

Carol was gazing out at the rain, silvered by the lights of passing vehicles, when she heard the roar of an engine and then the sound of skidding tires, followed by a shout. Recognizing Hal's voice, Carol, followed by Leota, ran out into the downpour.

"Jesus!" Hal was white faced. "That son of a bitch almost got Jill!"

Jill, shivering, allowed herself to be led back into the restaurant. The valet, umbrella aloft, waved his other hand in agitation. "Shall I call the police, sir?"

"There's no point. The SOB is long gone."

As soon as she was sure Jill was okay, Carol went back to Hal. "What happened?"

He'd calmed down. "Somebody drunk, I'd say. Nearly sideswiped the car, just as Jill was getting in the driver's side. If she hadn't looked up and realized what was happening, he would have hit her."

"You didn't get a number?"

He shook his head. Turning to the valet, who was hovering anxiously, he said, "Did you see anything?"

"No, sir, I'm sorry. It's wet, and it was just a dark car."

Carol and Leota waited until Jill said she was fine to drive, and they said their good-nights again, this time in a much more subdued manner.

Driving back to the hotel, Leota said, "I can't imagine that Jill has any enemies."

"Are you saying that was deliberate?" asked Carol, who'd already had the unsettling thought that Hal might have been too quick to dispense with his bodyguard.

"It probably was a drunk." She put a hand on Carol's knee. "Let's talk of other things."

Carol had asked that French champagne be left in an ice bucket in her room. They saluted each other solemnly. Carol felt pleasantly keyed up, as though she were about to run a race she knew she would win.

"Don't drink any more," said Leota. "I don't want any of your senses dulled."

"There's not much hope of that." Carol put down her champagne glass and stared into Leota's dark eyes.

"Tired?" said Leota. "It's almost midnight."

"No," said Carol. A slow fire glowed at her center. "I've never been more awake."

She looked at Leota's mouth, at her lips curved in a half-smile. "What now?"

"Now it begins," Leota said. "Don't be impatient, Carol. Let me take you there carefully, scrupulously, inexorably."

"You're all words," said Carol, suddenly breathless. "How about some action?"

They moved together for a luscious, honeyed kiss. Carol thought of slow-burning fires, of furnaces banked to keep in the heat. "I feel I could kiss you forever."

She slid her hand into the opening of Leota's shirt. Leota seized her fingers. "No, Carol, not yet. We have to kiss much more before you earn that privilege."

"How long?"

"I'll let you know."

Leota's mouth was delicious, her tongue soft, yet subtly demanding. Carol said against her lips, "Okay, I'll play it your way for now, but then it must be mine."

"It's a deal."

They kissed until Carol began to chafe under the restriction, to burn to touch Leota's skin, and to be touched in return.

Just as she was about to voice her demands, Leota said, "Will you undress me?"

"At last," said Carol, laughing.

"But take your time."

"I don't think I can."

"Please. You must."

Carol unbuttoned Leota's silver shirt, undid her bra, slid her hands over the coffee skin, and was rewarded with a gasp. "You're growing eager?" Carol said.

"Just a little, but I can wait."

Leota stepped out of her skirt, slipped off her shoes, let Carol slide her black underwear down her hips.

Carol bent her head to kiss Leota's erect nipples. "You're gorgeous," she said.

"My turn," said Leota, pushing Carol's head gently away.

Submitting to a leisurely undressing when she was throbbing with urgent desire was a delightful torture. Carol growled, deep in her throat.

Naked, they embraced. Carol felt burnished to a high polish, glowing with golden passion. Leota released her, took her hand. "To bed?"

Carol wanted to make a smart reply, but all she said was "Yes, and quickly."

"We have all night."

As they sank onto the sheets, Carol caught sight of their bodies in the mirror — brown skin against white, blond hair against black. The contrast was a charge, an electric kick that lifted her up another notch. "Look at us," she said.

"I don't want to look. I want to feel and taste."

Gradual, deliberate, her hand slow, her skin scorching hot, Leota stoked, stroked, brought Carol to the brink again and again, only to let her fall back every time. "God, this is agony," Carol murmured.

"This time," said Leota. "This time."

Carol surrendered to the mouth, the fingers, the will that held her transfixed. She was burning fiercely, her body consumed, her heart bursting.

"Now, Carol."

Obediently her body shattered the barrier, rose up to shudder with the exultation of release, of joy achieved. Carol thrilled to her own shout of triumph.

She was content, slippery with sweat, laughing with pleasure as her breathing slowed.

Leota lay watching her, smiling. "What do you think of my way, now?"

"Not bad," said Carol, "but surely we need a comparison." She propped herself on one elbow. "Brace yourself," she said. "We're going to try it my way."

CHAPTER THIRTEEN

Leota was caught up with the Rackham investigation, so late on Sunday afternoon Jill drove Carol back to Quantico. The FBI's hope that the lid could be kept on the discovery of Sir Richard's body had proved futile. By Sunday morning every news outlet was showing views of the desolate field where his body had been found; the children who'd discovered the corpse were enjoying their fifteen minutes of fame; the British Prime Minister had given a media conference expressing his shock and disbelief; and speculations that had been raised by various media pundits when Rackham had first disappeared were being re-hashed, tweaked, and offered to the public all over again.

Predictably, Sir Richard's wife was regarded by the media as a valuable quarry, and she hadn't been able to avoid a reporter and photographer getting into her hotel room by disguising themselves as hotel staff. Furious, Jill had taken Michele up to the suite for better protection and had spent most of day with her.

The traffic on the Beltway was heavy, requiring Jill's concentration, and since she clearly didn't feel like talking, they sat in companionable silence.

Carol's thoughts tumbled over one another: the coverage of Sir Richard's death; his wife's possible involvement; the near-miss at the restaurant last night that could have injured, or killed, Jill; Mike Yench's death, which, in the light of this murder, might not have been an accident.

And, of course, overlaid were the images Carol had of Leota — the sensations, scents, textures of last night's lovemaking. If Leota's way had been tormentingly deliberate, Carol's had been ferociously ardent. She smiled as she remembered the state of the bed after they'd thrashed together, turbulent, consuming each other in total abandonment.

In the morning they'd breakfasted together, quiet and spent. Carol hadn't asked Leota if there was, or had been, anyone important in Leota's life. If Leota chose to tell her, then that was fine, but Carol was determined to keep this light and easy. In her deep relationships she'd experienced happiness and gut-wrenching pain. This time she was playing it for laughs, at least for now. If something more developed, she'd worry about it later.

When they reached the Academy, Jill got out of the car to give her a hug. "Back to school, Carol."

Carol sighed. "I'm afraid so, but I think I'd rather be here, than in Washington."

Jill made a face. "It's pretty rough, but it's going to get rougher. Hal's flying back to LA tomorrow, but since the FBI has asked Michele to stay, I told her I'd keep her company." She looked hopefully at Carol. "Look, if you get bored, or can get some time off, I'd love to see you."

"It's a deal. We have every weekend free, so if you're still around next Saturday, we can get together."

Jill slid back behind the wheel. Carol said, "Be

very careful, please, especially when you're driving."

Jill looked up at her. "You're thinking of what happened at the restaurant, aren't you?"

"I'm thinking that if Hal has a bodyguard in Los Angeles, why not have one here, too?" She patted Jill's shoulder through the window. "That said, it probably was someone who'd had too much to drink."

As Jill waved and drove off, Carol asked herself why she hadn't seen it before. In the dark and rain, and with her newly blonded hair, at a distance Jill could be mistaken for Carol.

That was a sobering thought — that she might be a target, and that she had no idea why.

The evening meal had become the informal meeting time for the group, everyone having fallen into the routine of sitting together at the same table, and although people had moved around the first few meals, eventually everyone settled in one position. Carol knew it was absurd, but she had "her" seat, and felt proprietary about it.

Sunday evening had an informal air. The dining room was half empty, and the choice of food was restricted. Only four people besides herself were at their table — Peter Karfer, Ian Forteys, Nikki Lee, and Farid Sukani. No one sat in Mike Yench's position, and Carol was very aware of the empty place.

She looked around the table. Karfer was chatting to Nikki about ice hockey, and she was showing every evidence of boredom; Sukani was devouring the contents of his heaped plate with single-minded enthusiasm; and Ian Forteys was slumped in his chair across from her, his face drawn in fretful lines. He hadn't shaved, and the stubble of his beard was very dark against his sallow skin.

Tapping his thin fingers on the edge of the table, he said to Carol, "Do you know where Debra is? I expected her back by now."

"I've no idea. She went up to Washington with Agent Pyke, didn't she?"

"I rented a car and tried to find her, but she wasn't in the hotel she said she'd booked."

This was getting close to stalking, Carol thought. "Sorry," she said, "can't help you."

He nodded slowly, resentment clouding his face. "I never thought you would."

"Carol!" Peter Karfer was leaning toward her. "What do you think about Rackham, dead all these weeks? Who did him in?"

"I'm sure you've seen the news," said Carol. "Choose any story — there're enough of them."

"And what does Agent Woolfe think?"

"I've no idea."

"I think they should look at Mike's death again," said Nikki. "He worked with Sir Richard in London on drug initiatives. Looks more than a coincidence to me that they're both dead."

Carol went to get herself a coffee. Looking back at the table, she considered what motives there could be to want Yench out of the way. Sukani she could eliminate immediately, because he hardly knew Yench. Forteys clearly hated him and held a grudge because he believed Yench had persuaded Debra Caulfield to break the relationship with Forteys and stay in London. Nikki's complaint about Yench was the same as Carol's — he'd made uncouth advances.

The other person who had reason to want harm to come to Yench was Debra Caulfield. She seemed convinced he was setting her up to take the blame for the Rackham situation.

Making her way back to the others, Carol was again jolted by the thought that Mike Yench's death could have been a hit. What if there was a contract out on him? Of course, it would take some planning to kill him at the FBI Academy unless — she smiled to herself — the hit man was a fed. She could almost enjoy the far-fetched scenario she was creating. Frank Vertelle as a hitman? She'd love it to be him, just to get away from the drone of his irritating voice. Nancy Pyke had never, so far as Carol was aware, met Yench, but of course this shouldn't preclude her from tracking him down and dispatching him. Then again, it could be an agent she hadn't even met.

And there was Leota Woolfe . . .

* * * * *

It was back to schedule on Monday. Carol surveyed her classmates as they wandered into the lecture room. Debra Caulfield came in with Nikki Lee, who was describing in detail how she'd spent the weekend at Rehoboth Beach, Delaware. Debra Caulfield had been amused when Carol told her before breakfast about the fruitless search for her that Forteys had embarked upon in Washington. "I knew it!" she'd said. "That's why I changed hotels."

Carol had been curious about how Debra had got on with Nancy Pyke, and Debra had shrugged. "She was pleasant enough, but we both knew she was there to keep an eye on me and gain my confidence." Debra had showed her excellent teeth in a rare full smile. "She achieved the first, and not the second."

As the last person arrived, Frank Vertelle stalked into the room, his expression forbidding. On his way to the front of the room Harris asked him a question, and he snapped a bad-tempered answer.

Peter Karfer, who'd been in an aggravatingly boisterous mood at breakfast, demanded loudly, "Didn't you get any this weekend, Vertelle?"

There was a ripple of laughter, and Vertelle's eyes narrowed, but he ignored Karfer's remark. "This morning's sessions," Vertelle said in a monotone, "will cover developments in communications."

Vertelle's mood didn't improve as the day went on. He snapped at the inoffensive Sukani, spoke viciously to Nikki when she made a humorous remark about spy satellites, and, in a practical session, openly mocked Karfer's attempts to operate an electronic bug sweeper. His greatest ire, however, was directed at Carol. She had no idea what had provoked his animosity, but he seemed to be deliberately goading her for some reason, and so she kept her own temper in check.

Late in the afternoon Vertelle surrendered the lectern to a woman who looked like everybody's ideal of a favorite aunt. She had a sweet face, graying brown hair badly styled, and a comfortable, plump body. "I'm Hazel Byrd," she said in a mild voice that matched her expression.

She flipped open a folder. "Now, as you're no doubt aware, the chances of two people having an identical DNA profile are on the order of a hundred million to one."

Then she launched into a detailed analysis of the latest developments in DNA profiling. The implications for law enforcement swiftly became apparent to everyone in the room. "Traditional DNA fingerprinting requires at least five hundred to a thousand body cells from the subject," she said, "but a new method requires only a single cell."

She held up a forefinger. "Think of that, ladies

and gentlemen. One single human cell. That means positive identification can be made from one skin cell from a gun grip, one single sperm, one tongue cell on a licked stamp, one cell flaked from the scalp of a criminal.

She beamed at them. "I see you understand how important this is to crime detection. In the case of gang rapes, for example, the old method is useless, since a mixture of semen cannot be DNA typed. But with this process, single sperm cells can be separated and tested, providing evidence that will implicate every person involved in the sexual assault."

She went on to explain the process in detail, explaining how the single cell had its DNA copied until there was sufficient to identify the seven genetic markers that were used to create the unique genetic fingerprint.

Carol stifled a yawn. She'd slept badly, and the room was stuffy. She found her eyes almost irresistibly closing, and she had to fight hard not to fall asleep. In fact, she did doze for a moment, jerking herself awake when Vertelle's grating voice announced the end of the session. Carol picked up her notebook and stood up, ready to leave.

"Well, Ashton," said Vertelle loudly, "that was obviously far too complicated for you to comprehend, since you slept through most of the lecture."

Carol had had enough of him. "What exactly is your problem?" she said.

His narrow face reddened. "My problem is that I have to deal with second-rate officers like you."

Carol glared at him, tempted to say exactly what she thought, but unwilling to engage in a slanging match in front of her fascinated colleagues, who were clearly waiting to see what happened next.

"The rest of you leave," snarled Vertelle. "This is between Ashton and me."

"Do you know how ridiculous you sound?" said Carol.

Someone laughed, and Vertelle's face flushed an even deeper red. "Get out," he said, gesturing to the others. He pointed a quivering finger at Carol. "Except you."

Carol stood, hands on hips, while everyone else filed out. Peter Karfer was last, turning to say to Carol, "Would you like me to stay?"

"No, Peter, it's okay."

When the door closed, she swung around to Vertelle. She knew very well the nonconfrontational strategies she could use to defuse the situation, but she was damned if she was going to use them. "I can't imagine why you're singling me out," she said, "but I want to make it very clear to you I don't appreciate it. I expect to be treated in a professional manner, not yelled at as though I'm a school kid."

"You think you're special, do you?" he sneered. "I've met your type before."

"My type? What does that mean?"

"Don't think I don't know how you're trying to undermine my authority. I've been told what you've been saying about me."

Carol groaned to herself. Vertelle had obviously lost it and was in full paranoid mode. "I haven't been saying anything," she said, knowing that he wouldn't believe her.

"I'm going to make a formal report," he ground out, his eyes narrowed to slits.

"Good," said Carol. "You do that."

Outside the door, she found that several people had lingered. Ian Forteys gave her a sympathetic pat on the arm. "We'll back you up," he said. "Don't worry about that."

There was a murmur of agreement. "You should tell Agent Woolfe," said Karfer with a sly smile. "I'm sure *she'll* look after you."

She felt her face tighten at his insinuation, but decided one unpleasant confrontation a day was enough, so she filed the thought away that she would take the first good opportunity to make it very clear to Karfer that she wouldn't tolerate snide remarks about Leota or, for that matter, about anything else.

"Thanks for your support, everyone," she said, "but I'm sure that by tomorrow it will have all blown over."

"I'd rip his balls off," said Debra with a savagery that caused surprised looks.

Forteys gave a derisive grunt. "That's supposing that he *has* them," he observed.

CHAPTER FOURTEEN

Carol's run early on Tuesday morning was a delight. The cool air was like wine, the sunrise spectacular, and she felt in perfect harmony with gravity, running with an effortless stride that she felt she could keep up all day.

The experience was such a contrast to the

night before, when she'd still been smarting from Vertelle's unjustified attack. She'd been fed up with everyone and had kept to herself all evening, going for a brisk walk before bed, where she found herself rehearsing exactly what she'd say to Vertelle the next time she saw him.

The morning was so beautiful that she stayed out longer than usual, and when she went back to the dormitory most of her roommates were up and dressed. She grabbed her towel, toiletries, and cosmetic bag, intending to have a quick shower, but the unaccustomed weight of the bag caught her attention.

"What's that?" asked Robyn, yawning. She was one of the four other women in the room who were enrolled in the standard FBI eleven-week training course.

Puzzled, Carol said, "I'm not sure, I just found it in with my makeup, of all places."

Robyn examined the thin black cylinder in Carol's fingers. "I know what it is," she announced. "A collapsible truncheon. It extends to about twelve or so inches."

Carol played with the device until, with a twist, she pulled it out to its full length. She'd seen truncheons that folded in on themselves so they could be conveniently stowed in a pocket or in a holster, but never one quite so finely constructed. Made of some synthetic material, it had a matte surface. She hefted it in her hand. It would make a potent night stick, with enough whippiness in the shaft to deliver an extremely painful, even fatal, blow.

"A present from a secret admirer?" Robyn asked.

"I've no idea." Carol frowned over the deadly-looking little truncheon. Perhaps it was someone's idea of a joke, but if so, it was lost on Carol.

Debra came back from the bathroom. "What's that?"

Carol showed it to her. "It isn't yours, is it?"

"I've never seen it before."

Thinking that perhaps it had been put in her things by mistake, Carol polled the room, but nobody claimed the truncheon. She debated what to do with it, finally collapsing the device to its smallest size and stuffing it into a zip-up compartment in her suitcase.

The moment Carol walked into the dining hall she knew, from the odd tension in the buzz of subdued conversation, that something had happened. She had only to wait a moment to find out what it was, as Peter Karfer spotted her and rushed over. "Carol, you'll never guess what's happened. Vertelle's dead!"

Totally astonished, she stared at him. "What happened?"

"All I know is that they found him lying in the backseat of his car."

"Got to be suicide," said Debra, joining them with Nikki following. "Or, since Vertelle was such a toxic little swine, maybe his body just finally self-destructed."

There was a sudden hush as a phalanx of conservatively dressed individuals, led by Nancy Pyke, entered the hall. "FBI agents on the rampage," said Karfer. "When it's one of their own, they're bull terriers."

"It's pit bulls in the States," said Nikki. "Get it right for once, Pete."

Nancy Pyke's amplified voice rang out, "Attention, ladies and gentlemen. Please finish your breakfast by eight-fifteen. At that point you are to go directly to the location of your first scheduled session. Until further notice, no person is to return to dormitories or visit other areas."

A burst of noise followed this instruction. "Why are we doing this?" someone yelled.

"There has been a fatality," said Agent Pyke. "You will be asked if you have any objection to having your belongings searched."

"Well there's your answer," said Nikki. "Vertelle didn't suicide — he was murdered."

Pyke herself came to their classroom. Her squat body seemed to radiate steely resolve. She looked them over as though they were specimens

153

to be assessed, then said, "Frank Vertelle was killed sometime last night. It was not an accident, nor did he take his own life. We have reason to believe that someone enrolled in this course is involved."

She waited until the exclamations that followed this statement died away. "You will be interviewed individually, and at that interview you will be asked to formally agree to a search of your belongings."

A thread of anxiety was unreeling in Carol. The planted truncheon was just too coincidental. When it was her turn for an interview, she would mention it straightaway.

"Carol Ashton," said Agent Pyke, "you're first."

Nancy Pyke, accompanied by an agent she introduced as Thomas Urday, conducted the interview in the same room where Carol had been questioned about Mike Yench. Carol looked at the mirror wall and wondered if Leota was behind it or if she was still in Washington. She devoutly hoped it was the former.

Looking up at the video camera mounted on the wall, she saw from its glowing red eye that it was recording. "Before we start," Carol said, "I want to tell you that I found something strange in my things this morning, and I have no idea how it got there."

Nancy Pyke's expression didn't change. "Will you give us permission to search your belongings?"

"Of course, but I want to explain —"

"You can explain later. Now, would you give an account of your movements yesterday."

"*All* day?" Carol smiled, trying to establish a personal relationship with Agent Pyke.

When Carol questioned suspects she had often observed their attempts to win her over, and she had no compunction about doing exactly the same herself, even though she knew very well that the FBI agent would know exactly what she was trying to achieve.

"All day," said Pyke, her expression blank.

This was rapidly becoming a nightmare. Carol recounted the events of her day, agreeing that the final session of the course had ended with a verbal confrontation between herself and Vertelle.

She was asked to go through her actions from that point. Carol wanted to ask, "What was the time of death?" but knew that the agents wouldn't give any indication of when Carol might need an alibi.

Apart from the evening meal, Carol hadn't spent much time with anyone after the class had ended. She'd watched television for a while in the lounge with a couple of people she didn't know, and had then gone for a stroll before she went to bed.

"When you went for this stroll," said Agent Urday, his tone subtly suggesting that he doubted she'd done any such thing, "what route did you take?"

"I take a walk almost every night, if it isn't too cold."

"Your route last night, please."

Carol explained how she'd wandered in the direction of the library, circled it, then continued on toward the administration buildings before returning to the dormitory.

There was a knock at the door, a whispered consultation, and then Agent Pyke left the room. In a few moments she was back. "Stand up, please."

Carol got to her feet and then realized, with absolute incredulity, that Nancy Pyke was reading her the rights that any person arrested must be given. In an instant Urday had her hands behind her and was fastening handcuffs.

"You're arresting me?"

"For the murder of Federal Agent Frank Vertelle."

CHAPTER FIFTEEN

An hour had passed, and Carol was still seated in the interview room, her shoulders aching from the unaccustomed position her handcuffed wrists forced her to assume.

At first she'd protested, "Why do I have to be handcuffed? There're two of you. Besides, I'm not a threat to anyone."

Nancy Pyke had given her a grim smile. "Tell that to Vertelle and Yench."

"Mike Yench? I had nothing to do with his death."

"Coincidental, don't you think?" Pyke had said. "Two men dead within less than a week, both with head injuries? If you'd stopped at Yench, you might have got away with it, but now —"

"I had nothing to do with either one!"

Hearing the note of passionate sincerity in her own voice, Carol thought fleetingly of the many times she had interrogated a suspect who had had just that sound of candor and outraged innocence, but had later turned out to be guilty.

Carol had explained how she'd found a black cylinder in her makeup bag, and how she'd discussed it with Robyn, who'd identified it as a collapsible truncheon.

Nancy Pyke had been unimpressed, remarking, "A cover story in case a search was made."

She'd leaned forward, her face hard, "The weapon has been sent to our laboratories in Washington, along with the clothes you were reported wearing. If you paid attention in the lecture yesterday, Ashton, you'll know that tiny traces of DNA can be identified, even if an attempt has been made to clean the weapon. I fully expect that the results will show DNA from both victims."

She'd leaned back. "And with your fingerprints on the truncheon, it's an open-and-shut case."

"I've explained that I handled it."

"You've got an explanation for everything, haven't you, Ashton? Next you're going to be saying that someone is setting you up."

It was exactly what Carol had been thinking, but now it sounded weak, even to her. With growing dread, she realized that not only was it likely that someone had deliberately incriminated her, but that it had been done effectively. She had no firm alibi for either death, and she had little doubt that DNA testing of the truncheon would prove positive.

"I want a lawyer," she'd said.

"You have a name?"

"Hal del Bosco."

Nancy Pyke's lip had curled. "Hal del Bosco, is it? If you have the cash, you can buy your freedom, no matter what you do. You've got a lot of money, have you, Ashton? You're going to need it."

Then she'd jerked her head at Urday, and they'd both left the room, leaving Carol alone.

It was a technique Carol had often used herself. Leaving a subject isolated, with nothing to do, no one to talk to, just blank time to contemplate the worst that could happen. Anxiety, fear, and even panic inevitably rose in the suspect as the time dragged on and on. Then they'd be thirsty and hungry or need to use a bathroom — all additional pressures designed to soften up a suspect.

Carol glanced at her reflection in the mirror. She looked surprisingly unruffled, considering the anger and alarm that filled her. She knew that she was being observed from behind the glass, and she repressed a sudden childish desire to make a face at the unseen watchers. They were probably drinking coffee. She swallowed, thinking she could almost taste the hot, caffeine-loaded liquid.

Where was Leota? Surely not behind the mirror, watching Carol's interrogation. Carol bit her lip, wishing that by sheer will power she could bring Leota here. But of course she was still in Washington, deeply involved in the investigation of Rackham's death.

The minutes dragged by. Carol felt she knew the room intimately — the bland walls, the utilitarian metal table bolted to the floor, the unyielding surface of the beige plastic chairs, all illuminated in the flat light glaring down from four glass panels in the ceiling. Because it was usually used as a training facility, the walls and furniture were in much better condition than most interrogation rooms Carol had seen. And the air-conditioned air smelled clean, not filled with the smells of disinfectant and sweaty fear.

She forced herself to calm down and think logically. Who could possibly have set her up this way, and why? Someone who had access to the dormitory, obviously. Debra Caulfield slept in the same room, but that might mean nothing. The doors were never locked, so anyone at the Academy could walk in unchallenged.

Could it be a sick joke? Perhaps the truncheon hadn't been used to murder anyone, and there was no incriminating DNA on it. Then the FBI labs would come up empty and she'd be released for lack of evidence, and the worst would be that someone would have a good laugh at her expense.

She shook her head, knowing it wasn't a joke. Was it that someone hated her, or that she was merely a handy distraction for the feds to pursue? A chill touched her as she contemplated the bitter malice behind the actions. If Mike Yench had been deliberately slain, then this was a person who could coolly wait four days, then kill again. And take the precautionary step of incriminating someone else. She could see the faces of her classmates — was it one of them? Someone who sat in the dining hall, shared a joke, attended classes — and carried a tidy, easily concealed weapon.

Stiff from the awkward stance her bound hands forced her to keep, Carol got up and walked around the room, stretching her arms behind her. The handcuffs were tight on her wrists, and she was filled with a sudden desire to get them off, whatever it took. She couldn't stand being restricted, not having any control over what she did and where she went.

"Sit down, please."

Nancy Pyke was back. She came into the room alone, shutting the door firmly behind her. "Let's have little talk, Carol," she said. She gestured at the video camera. "This is just between us, nothing's being recorded."

Until this point, Pyke had used "Ashton" to refer to Carol. The use of her first name signaled that the agent was changing her tactics.

Carol said, "I don't believe I have to answer any more questions until my legal representative is present."

Nancy Pyke's mouth sketched a smile. "We're just having a talk, that's all. Then I might be able to have those handcuffs removed. And perhaps you'd like coffee, and to freshen up in the restroom?" She paused to let the offer of these comforts sink in. "So let's have a chat, shall we, Carol? Then I'll see what I can do for you."

Carol could almost smile at Agent Pyke playing nice cop, but the offer to have her handcuffs off was almost overwhelmingly tempting. And coffee . . .

Refusing to even think about these seductive offers, Carol said, her tone as reasonable as she could make it, "The truncheon you found in my suitcase was planted. I've never seen it before. If it turns out to be the murder weapon, then someone is deliberately incriminating me. And before you ask, I don't know who, or why."

Pyke nodded affably. "That's an interesting scenario."

"Does it occur to you that only a total idiot would keep a murder weapon where it could easily be found and would even display it to someone else?"

Pyke raised her heavy shoulders. "Perhaps you felt invincible and believed no one could touch you because what you'd done was right." She paused, then added persuasively, "That's what you thought, isn't it? That they both deserved to die?"

Carol sighed. "I had nothing to do with it, and, apart from the planted truncheon, there's no evidence to connect me to these deaths."

"I don't believe you have an alibi for either," Pyke observed.

"What times would that cover?" asked Carol quickly.

"No, Carol, I can't tell you that," said Pyke with an indulgent smile. "That would be entirely too helpful."

Carol wriggled her shoulders. She could visualize herself only a few hours before, running with uncomplicated pleasure in the cool morning air, feeling in harmony with nature.

Nancy Pyke leaned her elbows on the table. "You can tell me," she said pleasantly. "I understand all about men and how they are."

Carol tingled with impatience. She was exasperated by this woman's questions; she was tired of the interrogation, and she wanted more than anything to get out of this room.

"Just between us," Nancy Pyke went on in a confiding tone, "I've often wanted to hurt them myself."

"Perhaps you should have counseling," said Carol helpfully.

Pyke's demeanor changed. Narrowing her eyes, she said, "You think this is funny, do you? You won't be laughing when we transfer you to the nearest correctional facility. In fact I'd say you'll be crying — crying quite a lot. A woman like you, they'll eat you up."

Carol sat back. If she'd been able, she would have crossed her arms. "I believe our little chat is over," she said.

"It's because you're a lesbian, isn't it? A ball-breaking, man-hating lesbian. You despise men, want to destroy them. Yench came on to you, and you were revolted, sickened."

The agent's voice rose as she warmed to her theme. "Did he laugh at you, Ashton? Call you ugly names? You couldn't stand that, and breaking his knee cap wasn't enough, was it? So later you found him and you hit him, hard as you could, then covered it up as an accident."

When Carol looked at her, stony faced, Pyke got to her feet. "Frank Vertelle was my colleague and my friend. I know his wife and his children, back in Atlanta. I won't rest until you pay for his murder."

Carol raised her eyebrows. "And my motive was . . . ?"

"Everyone in the course heard the vicious fight you had with Agent Vertelle. Here was another man taking advantage of you, humiliating you. It seemed you'd got away with murder before, so you stalked him and beat his head in. You were in a frenzy. How many times did you hit him? Three? Four times?"

She paused, waiting for Carol to respond. When she remained silent, Nancy Pyke went on in a much milder tone, "So why don't you confess, Carol, and save us all a lot of trouble? It'll pay off if you do. For one thing, I'm sure you'll get a lighter sentence."

Bullshit!

Carol's response was so immediate that she believed for a moment that she had spoken the word aloud. Apparently her face had conveyed the thought quite clearly, because Nancy Pyke glowered at her.

"If you won't cooperate," she snapped, "then I can do nothing for you. I'll arrange for you to be taken to suitable confinement while our investigations continue."

The door opened, and Agent Urday put his head in, saying to Pyke, "Do you have a moment?"

With a final glare at Carol, she left the room.

There was another long wait. Carol walked around, sat down, got up, and walked around

165

again. She imagined what it would be like to be in a cell with an open toilet bowl and hard bunk bed. Would she be by herself or forced to share it with one or more other women? She could picture the bars, the hard floor, the noises, the smells, the lack of privacy. Suddenly the dormitory situation at the Academy seemed more than acceptable.

Her next thought must have resonated in countless suspects' minds: *This can't be happening to me.*

She flexed her knees, suddenly grateful that she at least could walk unimpeded. She vividly remembered American news shots of accused criminals shackled at the ankles so that they could only take tiny steps, their handcuffed hands linked by chain to metal bands around their waists. Surely that only was done with the most desperate felons, the ones most likely to try to escape — not someone like her.

She was at such a disadvantage, grappling with a system she didn't fully understand. It was a comfort to think of Hal del Bosco. Hal would know what to do. He was probably back in Los Angeles by now, but he must know someone who could stand in for him and look after her interests. Carol was hazy about United States law — she understood that the murder of a federal officer was a federal offense, but was there bail for murder in this situation? And could she raise it? She'd seen the gigantic sums that high-profile murder suspects in this country had to put up to get out on bail.

She spun around at the sound of the door opening. Urday came in. "Your wrists, please."

Carol looked over her shoulder, hardly daring to believe it, as he unlocked the cuffs.

"Thank you," she said, rubbing her wrists.

"Don't thank him," said Leota from the doorway. "Thank me."

CHAPTER SIXTEEN

Carol wrapped her hands around the plastic cup. Its warmth comforted her, and the coffee tasted glorious. The canteen was nearly empty, and she and Leota shared a table in a corner as far as possible from anyone else.

Leota played with a packet of sugar. "Nancy Pyke overstepped her authority."

"I'm delighted you outrank her."

"I do, Carol, but this may be a temporary reprieve."

This wasn't a surprise, but Carol still felt a jolt. "You think I'll be arrested again after the lab tests are completed on the truncheon?"

"It's a possibility, particularly if it is the weapon used to kill Vertelle."

"I'm sure it is," said Carol. "Otherwise, there'd be no point in planting it on me." She smiled at Leota. "I've never been so pleased to see anyone in my life. How did you know Pyke had arrested me?"

"I was on my way back to Quantico when I got the message on my cell phone."

"Agent Pyke told you what she was doing?"

Her remark drew a derisive laugh. "Hardly. Nancy's too ambitious to let anyone know what she's up to. She was determined to break you, then take all the kudos for solving the murder of a federal officer. It would have been very good for her career, so it's a pity you didn't cooperate."

"Then who told you?"

Leota frowned at Carol's persistence. "Nikki Lee did."

"She's an informant."

Leota shifted in her seat, hiding a yawn. "I'm sorry, I've been up most of the night. About Nikki, you should be pleased that she contacted me. I'd intended to do a couple of errands, but when she called I came straight to the Academy."

Reflexively, Carol looked at her wrists. Both had a faint red bracelet where the handcuffs had chafed her skin. "I'd hate to think how long I'd have been in that room if you hadn't."

"I'm sorry you were there as long as you were, but once I arrived and found they'd turned up a possible murder weapon in your belongings, I did a little investigating of my own. You'll be pleased to know that your mate, Robyn Talus, said that she saw you discover the truncheon, and when you did, you showed what she judged to be genuine surprise. I imagine it was wiped clean before it was put there, so it helps that Robyn also said that you were the only person she saw handle the thing, which explains why your fingerprints are on it."

Carol played back the scene in her imagination. "There were other people around, but I remember Debra Caulfield. She came back from the bathroom and saw me with it."

"Debra confirmed she saw the truncheon, but she also said that you seemed familiar with the weapon."

Carol looked at her sharply. "Familiar?"

"From the way that you were holding it, and the way you collapsed it down to its smallest size before you put it away."

"Doesn't sound like she was trying to help me, does it?"

Leota cocked her head. "Not noticeably."

"I need to know everything you can tell me about both deaths."

"Carol, you're not playing detective over this. You're out of your league outside your own country."

"God!" said Carol, suddenly angry. "This happens to be my life and liberty at stake here. So don't hold out on me."

Leota put up a hand. "Okay, okay. You win."

After she left Leota, Carol called Jill's hotel to get Hal's office number in Los Angeles, telling Jill vaguely that she needed legal advice on a matter. She knew that Jill was coping with both Michele Rackham's emotions and the media assault, and at this point Carol wasn't going to add more to her concerns.

After she'd jotted the number down, she said, "How's Michele?"

"She's falling to pieces. Hold on for a minute..." Jill was back in a few moments. "I've closed the door so she can't hear."

"I know she must be grieving. If she's very upset, perhaps a doctor —"

"You don't understand. It's not grief, it's fear. And guilt." Jill paused, then said, "Carol, I think she might have done it."

"Done what?"

"Her husband's murder. I don't mean for one moment she killed him herself. I mean that she paid someone to do it. Identifying his body did it. She's unraveling, right in front of my eyes. And she's said so many things to me that are incriminating about the hit man and —"

"Have you told Hal?"

"Yes, of course. He says to sit tight and do nothing. He's flying in tomorrow."

Carol put down the receiver feeling nonplussed. That Rackham's wife might be his murderer had never seemed a real possibility. She could see Michele Rackham's heart-shaped face, her prominent nose, her awkward stance. She could hear her half swallowed English vowels as she'd said to Carol in Jill and Hal's living room, "The authorities are badgering me, you know, but I can't imagine what I'm supposed to have done with him."

And all the time, thought Carol acerbically, it was obvious that she *could* imagine exactly what had happened to Sir Richard.

She called Hal's office number hoping to speak with him, but he wasn't available, so she had to be content with leaving a message for him to call her back.

Then, finding herself ravenous because she'd missed lunch, she gobbled down junk food from a vending machine. Then, assuming that sessions would have been canceled for the rest of the day, she went to the library and found a quiet desk

172

away from the main traffic in the building. She'd deliberately avoided her classmates, as she was sure they would have heard about her arrest and subsequent release, and she was feeling too wrung out to cope with their questions and comments.

She took out paper and her gold fountain pen and laid them on the desk in front of her. If she'd been in Sydney, Carol would have had Mark Bourke available to draw up one of his neat diagrams on a whiteboard, but this time she would have to make do with paper and ink.

The times of death Leota had given her were of very little help. Mike Yench had been unconscious, his brain hemorrhaging, for some time before he succumbed. If it were murder — the autopsy results were being reviewed to see if this could be established — his killer was long gone by the time Yench had died, which was somewhere between nine and eleven P.M. Carol had been the last person to report seeing him alive, around six o'clock.

Frank Vertelle had been attacked next to his car, which had been located in a remote corner of a parking lot. Any results were very preliminary, but there was no doubt about murder. He'd been struck at least three times with great force, and his assailant had dragged his body into the backseat of the car, covering it with a blanket from the trunk. Vertelle's death had probably been almost instantaneous, and body temperature taken at the scene had given a rough estimate that set the attack at somewhere between seven and nine-thirty on Monday morning.

"Which covers some of the time you were out walking," Leota had observed. "That's why, once the weapon was found in your possession, Nancy Pyke was sure she had the right person."

"How much blood?"

She knew the FBI lab wouldn't find Vertelle's blood on her clothes, so she was hoping that there had been considerable splatter, indicating that the real murderer must have traces on his or her clothes.

Leota had shaken her head. "I know what you're hoping, but there wasn't a great deal of blood. The truncheon is almost certainly the weapon, by the way. It's neat and deadly, and can be used with tremendous force concentrated in a small area of contact."

Carol uncapped her pen. There were three incidents to consider. Yench's death, which might remotely still be an accident; the incident outside the restaurant, which for present purposes she would assume had targeted her, not Jill; the murder of Frank Vertelle.

She hadn't added the planting of the murder weapon to her mental list, because anyone could have done that. It would be slightly easier for a woman to walk into their room, but people were coming and going all the time, and the doors were never locked.

What was the link between Yench and

Vertelle? Unless there were two separate assailants, their murders were somehow related to each other. Although Carol was aware that the perpetrator was possibly someone she didn't know, whose motives were tied to Sir Richard Rackham's drug enterprise, all her instincts told her that the murderer was someone she saw every day. The time frames of the two deaths were such that any member of the class could have had a window of opportunity for each of them.

Carol wrote the names in alphabetical order: Debra Caulfield, Ian Forteys, Peter Karfer, Nikki Lee. After a moment's thought she added Harris and Sukani with question marks beside their names, thought about it, then crossed them out. It was too much of a stretch to believe they, or the other four members of the course, were implicated.

Doodling always helped Carol think, so she began to draw arrows and squares along the edge of the page, embellishing and shading as she went. She underlined Debra's name. She had an excellent motive to wish Mike Yench dead — the conviction that he was working to make sure she was the one to take the heat in the Rackham drug case. But Carol could think of no reason why Debra, even though she'd definitely been in Washington that night, would want to run her down. As for Vertelle, Debra, along with everyone else in the class, had experienced his cutting remarks and hostile behavior. Vertelle was unpleasant, but that hardly seemed to provide a convincing motive for his murder.

Carol could see Ian Forteys's thin, intense face in her mind's eye. He was another one with a fine motive to kill Yench. He'd openly said he hated him and had blamed him for the breakup of his relationship with Debra. He was in Washington over the weekend, looking for Debra. But again, why would he try to run Carol down? And regarding Vertelle, it was the same situation as Debra's.

Carol frowned, thinking about the course. Perhaps she hadn't noticed that Frank Vertelle was picking on someone more than the others, but it seemed to her he'd been an equal opportunity oaf, indiscriminately censuring his students.

Peter Karfer was next. He'd called Yench by his nickname, Magic Mike, and had introduced Yench and Debra Caulfield as his friends. Could he have been interested in Debra and seen Yench as a rival? Carol sorted through her memories, trying to isolate a look or an attitude that might support this hypothesis, but she could pinpoint nothing.

She was getting nowhere. She put down her pen and put her hands behind her head. Would Karfer aim a car at her? Peter made snide remarks, particularly about Leota, but then, he made similar remarks — ones that he no doubt thought witty — to everyone else, too.

Karfer as Vertelle's killer? Carol sighed with

irritation. Vertelle was the problem every time. She was willing to bet that most people in the class disliked him, but his type was hardly rare. And if everyone was feeling the lash of his contempt, then why would one individual be driven to lethal rage?

Last on the list was Nikki Lee. Carol liked Nikki, but put that to one side. She'd known several murderers she liked, but that had never influenced her wholehearted pursuit of them. Nikki clearly detested Yench, particularly after his unwelcome pass at her, but this didn't seem enough reason to kill him.

The irony didn't escape Carol: Nancy Pyke certainly thought that this was a good enough motive for Carol, so why couldn't it apply to Nikki as well?

She remembered that Nikki had said she'd spent the weekend at some beach resort in Delaware, and if that were true, then she couldn't have been outside the Washington restaurant on Saturday night. Carol put her pen down in disgust. She was willing to give this up altogether, to assign the incident to a drunk not driving too well.

She pictured Nikki beating in Frank Vertelle's skull. The out-of-control rage required didn't fit the woman she knew. Carol clicked her tongue. Who did she really know? With the exception of Peter, these were people she'd met only a few days ago.

Carol seized the page and crushed it into a ball. This was a waste of time. She tapped her forefinger against her lips, then smoothed out the paper. On the crumpled surface she wrote Nancy Pyke's name, hesitated, then added *Leota Woolfe*.

Deciding to disregard the restaurant incident, she tried out each name against the two victims. Nancy Pyke had no discernible motive to kill Yench and had said to Carol that Frank Vertelle was a colleague and a friend, although this was not necessarily true.

Leota? Carol knew she was unlikely to be impartial here, but she tried. The agent knew a great deal about the British cops. She had said specifically that Mike Yench was up to his neck in the drug trade and that Debra was involved with Rackham and had tipped him off. What if Leota was involved herself? What if Mike knew this and she had to shut him up?

Carol shifted uncomfortably in her seat. She didn't like thinking these things about the woman she'd made love with, even if her musings were pure conjecture. Carol knew it wasn't logical, but she felt shabby even to be considering that Leota might be involved.

She screwed up the paper again, and threw it with force into the nearest wastebasket.

CHAPTER SEVENTEEN

Wednesday morning heralded another crisp, beautiful day, and Carol felt restored to her usual self. Last night, exhausted by events, Carol had eaten her evening meal as early as possible, sitting at another table with strangers and evading any attempts at conversation. She knew the word must have spread that she was a suspect in the murder of an FBI agent, but no one said anything overt about the matter, and as soon as she'd eaten she escaped from the dining hall.

Carol had received a message that Hal was available, and called him, giving a brief summary of what had happened to her. He'd been very reassuring, promising to contact an excellent criminal lawyer in Richmond on her behalf. Carol hadn't said anything about Michele Rackham, and he'd volunteered nothing on the subject.

She felt hammered into the ground, so she'd gone to bed early and had pretended to be asleep when the others came in, listening to their chatter with sleepy inattention, until someone had remarked that with two murders at the Academy, it might be wise to lock the dormitory door. Debra's cool voice had replied, "But what if we lock the murderer in with us?"

Carol had contemplated sitting up and demanding, "Are you referring to me?" but had thought better of it. After all, why should Carol expect trust or loyalty from Debra Caulfield?

Now, in the morning light, she felt refreshed and ready to cope with whatever happened. Leota had told her that the DNA testing would take several days, so Carol felt she had at least a short time when her freedom was not in jeopardy.

When she picked up her messages after breakfast, she found one from Hal saying the lawyer he recommended would be pleased to represent her if it became necessary. Delightfully, there was also one from Leota, asking Carol to dine with her that evening at a restaurant outside the Academy. Carol left an enthusiastic yes on Leota's voice mail and went to class.

Electronic crime was the topic in the first session, and they had a new instructor, Rob Bane. He was a diffident, shyly smiling man who was the antithesis of Frank Vertelle.

"Nine hundred million people using the Internet," he began. "Can you imagine the scale of the offenses that can be committed on a global basis, anonymously, and at great speed? We need a coordinated international response to deal with electronic crime. Some of these don't involve new offenses, but rather new methods of executing them. Apart from child pornography, terrorism, racism, fraud, and money laundering, there are growing forms of e-crime, including cyber-stalking and political and industrial espionage."

Carol tried to absorb the information, but her attention kept wandering to the people about her. They all looked encouragingly normal: Peter Karfer had taken off his gold-rimmed glasses and was rubbing the bridge of his nose; Debra Caulfield's glossy dark head was held attentively as she took notes; Nikki Lee, grinning broadly, had bent her stocky body to whisper something to Harris, who was seated in the row in front of her; Ian Forteys, his chin resting on his steepled fingers, was listening closely to the lecturer.

During the coffee break, Carol struck up a conversation with Nikki and Ian Forteys.

"Hear you got yourself arrested," said Nikki, "and then Pyke had to let you go. That must have ruined her day."

"It seemed to," said Carol. "And Nikki, thank you for calling Leota Woolfe. That helped a lot."

"They searched all our rooms." Forteys was aggrieved. "Like we were common criminals."

"Whoever it is," Nikki grinned, "the person in question is an uncommon criminal." She put her hand on Carol's arm, "And it's not you, Carol. Everyone knows that." She looked around conspiratorially. "I'd say Debra would be a prime suspect."

Forteys's face hardened. "Watch your bloody mouth."

"I never watch my mouth," said Nikki. "It's part of my charm."

He grunted, and moved away. Looking after him, Carol said, "Ian didn't like Mike Yench or Vertelle. Why wouldn't he be your prime suspect?"

Nikki made a dismissive gesture. "He hasn't got the nerve."

"And Debra does?"

"Oh yes," said Nikki, "Debra does." She pursed her lips. "She's sharing a room with you, Carol. How easy it would be to plant something in your things."

"Do you know something concrete, Nikki, or are you just guessing?"

"Just guessing, but yesterday, when you didn't come back from your interview with Pyke, Debra couldn't wait to tell everyone about how she'd seen you in the dormitory waving a truncheon about."

"It's true, that did happen."

"Ah," Nikki replied, "but she said it with such relish."

Carol went back to the class thinking about Nikki. She was such an attractive personality, so much fun. But if one were a murderer, what better disguise could one have?

Leota picked her up at seven. Carol leaned back, relaxed, and watched Leota's profile as they drove to the little local restaurant that Leota had discovered. The food was good and plain. "Home-grown American," Leota said.

Over their first glass of wine, Leota said, "I've booked a room in a motel. Is that okay with you?"

Carol felt a primal thrill, dark and basic. "Very okay."

She looked at the woman across the table from her and tried to separate the person she knew intimately from her job as a federal agent. "I can't help feeling that all the while you have a hidden agenda," she said.

"Where you're concerned, I think my agenda is glaringly obvious."

Carol shrugged off the flippant remark. "Why were Debra Caulfield and Mike Yench sent to do this course?"

Leota hesitated, then said, "To isolate them from the action while we moved in on Rackham's organization."

"And Nikki Lee?"

"She's there to win confidences, feed back information."

"On me?"

"On anyone."

"And you? What about you?"

"Me?" Leota looked surprised. "I work for the FBI. I would have thought my position was obvious."

"Not so obvious to me," said Carol. "Are you investigating Hal and Jill?"

Clearly taken aback, Leota hesitated, then said, "How sharp you are, Carol. It's true I was assigned to gather intelligence on Hal del Bosco and some of his more notorious clients, but I'm happy to say that I had to report back that there was nothing to interest the FBI. With Hal, what you see is what you get."

Carol sat back and regarded her steadily. "I don't believe you," she said.

With a flash of anger, Leota said sharply, "I don't need this. I've been as frank as I could be with you — actually I've said more than I should."

"Where is the Rackham case in the scheme of things?"

"The biggest case of my career," said Leota simply.

Carol took a sip of wine. "Would you throw me to the wolves if it meant you could break the case?"

"I'd throw many people, believe me, but not you." She put a hand on Carol's. "I'd like you to believe me when say I haven't felt this way before."

"So there's no one special in your life?"

Releasing Carol's hand, Leota leaned back, considering her soberly. "I wondered when you'd ask. The answer is, there was once, but there is no longer. Is that satisfactory?"

Carol smiled at her. "For the moment."

The motel was nothing special, but clean and comfortable. "Best I could get on short notice," said Leota. "Can you cope?"

"Make it worth my while."

To kiss Leota was to taste honey and cinnamon, but with an astringent edge of uncertainty. Carol knew there was danger to any hard-won serenity she might have, but she willingly embraced the danger. "You're delicious," she breathed.

They kissed, spiraling down into raw sensation.

A noise cut into their sensuous cocoon. "Christ!" Leota fumbled in her bag, flipped open her cell phone. "Woolfe." She listened, then snapped, "I'll be there. Don't make a move until I arrive."

Carol sank down on the edge of the bed. "What is it?"

"I'm afraid I have to go."

"It's Michele Rackham, isn't it? You're going to arrest her."

Leota frowned at her. "What exactly do you know?"

"She hired a hit man to kill her husband. I imagine that he has talked."

"My God," said Leota. "I could really love you, you know."

Carol caught a taxi back to the Academy. She was tightly drawn and jumping with energy. Ideas were bouncing in her head. Suddenly, as if a current had flipped the pieces, she saw everything from a different perspective.

She went straight to the administration offices, finding one bored man on duty. "I want to see Nancy Pyke."

"She isn't available."

"It's urgent. My name is Carol Ashton. She'll want to see me."

She was kept waiting in a small office for an hour, and then a visibly annoyed Nancy Pyke turned up. Instead of her usual conservative suit, she wore jeans and a pullover. "Do you know what time it is? What the hell do you want?" she demanded, her voice harsh with antagonism.

"You're questioning everybody about Agent Vertelle's death."

"Of course. Is that what you've dragged me back here to ask?"

"Someone told him I was criticizing him behind his back, undermining his authority. Do you know who that was?"

The anger faded from Nancy Pyke's face. "Frank told me that himself," she said.

"Told you the name?"

She shook her head. "No. But I remember it was a man. Frank told me he went into graphic detail about what you'd said."

Not really expecting to convince her, Carol said, "It isn't true that I talked about Vertelle behind his back. Someone wanted to engineer a fight between us."

Nancy Pyke stepped up to Carol, her face set. "If you're playing games with me, I'll hang you out to dry."

"While you're wasting time with me, the real murderer is out there, free."

"You'd say that, whether you were guilty or not." Pyke spun on her heel to leave. She paused at the doorway to say caustically, "If you find this mythical murderer, be sure to tell me."

"Tomorrow," said Carol to her retreating back. "I'll tell you tomorrow."

Knowing there was no way she could go to sleep yet, Carol went into the dormitory building's lounge and joined a few other late-night people watching television. Images danced across the screen without her brain making any sense of them. Her thoughts churned. There were eight men in the class, but only two of them were likely to have lied to Vertelle about Carol. Ian Forteys and Peter Karfer.

She absently watched a commercial for an on-line broker while she examined the insight that had illuminated her thoughts. She'd been looking at things the wrong way, wondering who hated Yench and Vertelle, but it was who hated *her*. The planting of the truncheon wasn't just a clever ploy to deflect attention from the real murderer, it was a clear intention to trap Carol, to have her accused and found guilty of a capital crime.

The late night news came on, and Carol sat up when the announcer said, "Tonight, the sensational arrest of Sir Richard Rackham's widow on suspicion of procuring his murder. Sources tell us that a man is cooperating with the authorities."

With fascination, Carol saw Leota on the

screen, escorting a gray-faced Michele through a cordon of cameras and reporters.

Looking around, Carol realized she was the last one in the room. She flipped off the television and went to the door to turn off the main light.

"Hello, Carol," said Peter Karfer. "I've been waiting to get you alone. I saw you talking with Agent Pyke this evening, and that worried me. I can't let you worm your way out of a murder charge, so I'm thinking you might cement your guilt by fleeing. That would do it, don't you think?"

CHAPTER EIGHTEEN

The night was very dark, with an overcast sky and the hint of rain in the air. "We're going for a drive," said Karfer. "This is Vertelle's gun, by the way. Beretta, nine millimeter, with hollow-point rounds. Make a nasty mess of your guts."

He had an arm companionably around her as he jabbed the automatic hard into Carol's side.

"Did your friend Agent Woolfe tell you Vertelle's gun was missing? No? I wonder what else she didn't tell you."

Karfer's car was a dark blue sedan. "A nice, anonymous rental car," he said, gesturing for her to get behind the wheel.

"It was you who nearly ran Jill down."

"It was me. The rain made it hard to see, and I thought she was you. But it was only to scare you, so it didn't really matter."

Never get in a car. That was standard advice to anyone being abducted. Once inside a moving vehicle, a victim's chance of survival diminished considerably.

"Why would you want to scare me?" Carol asked, with effort keeping her voice in a friendly, conversational tone.

"Because I can. You're scared now, aren't you?"

She could feel the blood pumping hard through her veins, ready for fight. "Of course I am. Peter, don't do this."

"Don't bother playing for time. There's no one around. Get in the car." His teeth flashed in a smile. "And please don't think I won't use this gun, because I will, no worries. Picture it, Carol, you'll be down on the ground, vomiting blood, while I'm pressing your fingers onto the grip of the Beretta." He shook his head in mock regret. "Such a tragic suicide, and so messy."

Assessing her chances of disabling him whilst

deflecting the gun rammed into her ribs, Carol said, "You win."

Her words pleased him, as she intended they would. He pushed her into the car on the passenger's side. "Clamber over into the driver's seat, and don't try anything. I'm right beside you."

He got in after her, watching with amusement as she maneuvered over the center console. He handed her the keys. "Now, drive."

She started the car. The gates to the Academy had security. That would be her next best chance. As if reading her mind, Karfer said, "Don't try anything with the guard. If you do, I'll shoot him in the face, and then I'll kill you."

"Won't that mess up the suicide story?"

"I'll think of something, I always do."

She involuntarily gasped as he shoved the barrel savagely into her side. "Come on, Carol, get into your role. You asked to borrow my car for a midnight spin, and I said I'd come along too."

The guard at the gate was friendly. Checking their IDs, he said, "Late for you folks."

"You know how it is," said Karfer, winking at him. "No privacy at the Academy." He rested his left arm on Carol's shoulders. His right hand, hidden under his jacket, kept the gun pressing heavily against her. "Just looking for a little quality time together."

The guard grinned. "Right, I get the picture." He stepped back.

192

"Very good," said Karfer as they drove through. "We're heading for the Ninety-five."

"This is insane."

He made an impatient noise. "Of course it's not insane. That's what small-minded people say when they don't understand."

"What is there to understand? You killed Yench, and then you killed Vertelle."

"You see? You don't understand."

"Then explain it to me."

He laughed aloud, triumphant. "It was you, Carol, it was always *you*."

She gave him a quick glance. In the light from the dashboard the cleft in his chin was very noticeable. His full-lipped mouth was curved in an ironic smile.

"I was going to kill you in Sydney, but then the FBI course came up, and I thought, why not another country? A new challenge?"

A car horn blared. Carol wrenched her attention back to the road, and Karfer jammed the gun hard into her ribs. "You'll kill us both if you're not careful." His tone was jovial.

It was disorienting to have the steering wheel on the left, where in Australia the passenger would sit. "I'm not used to driving on this side of the road."

"Then concentrate. And don't think of putting on the hazard lights or flashing the headlights. I'll notice."

She risked another quick look at him. His

short sandy hair and his gold-rimmed glasses made him part of her ordered world, but inside that familiar skin was a stranger.

"I've been watching you for a long time," Karfer said, his voice booming in the enclosed space, "waiting until everything was just right. We'd meet now and then, and I'd know I had the power of life and death over you, just like I had over a bully called Shales at school. I executed him, and no one suspected anything. You can't imagine, of course, what's it's like."

"You feel like a god."

Karfer gave an amused snort. "Very good, Carol. You're trying hard, but, in the end, it won't make any difference."

They turned north onto the freeway, which, even at this hour, had traffic streaming in both directions. A light rain began to fall, and Carol fumbled around until she found the wipers. "Are we going to Washington?" she said.

"Oh no, we're going much farther than that. I've been scouting around, when I wasn't following you, and I believe I found the perfect place."

Carol looked at her hands, tight on the wheel. "The perfect place to kill me?"

"I hope so."

Carol felt a surge of rage. This wasn't going to happen to her. She said, "We're doing seventy — that's what, a hundred and ten kilometers an hour? If I ram something at this speed, I'd say we'll both be killed."

Karfer leaned over and undid her seat belt. "You'll definitely be killed," he said. He laughed softly. "But you won't do that, will you, Carol? You must be coming to the conclusion that your death is inevitable — and that I'm not a pervert and won't make you suffer. But you'll still hold out hope to the very end. Maybe you can escape. Maybe I'll change my mind. Maybe you can talk me out of it."

"The least you can do," said Carol, "is tell me why." Her eyes scanned constantly, looking for something, anything, that might give her an edge. Vehicles were all around her, people speeding to their safe homes, to their mundane destinations.

Karfer settled himself more comfortably in his seat. "Why you? Oh, you're such a golden girl, with everything you want. You always know the right people, pull the right strings. I've seen the attention you get, the way you're on television, in the newspaper. The famous, the wonderful, the adored Detective Inspector Carol Ashton."

"So this is merely professional jealousy, Peter?"

She winced as he jabbed the barrel into her ribs again. "All my life," he said, "it's been unfair. I haven't had the chances everyone else gets."

"You've done well."

He ignored her placatory remark. "I have more talent than you. I'm smarter and quicker, but that's never counted for much. You had everything handed to you on a plate, while I had to work bloody hard for it."

Aware of the futility of arguing with him, Carol said in a tone of polite inquiry, "And Yench and Vertelle? Where do they fit in?"

"Thinking on the fly, Carol, that's where the fun is. I've been watching constantly — you never realized, I know — and I saw Magic Mike come on to you, and how you crippled him, and I thought, *This is the beginning. This is where it all unfolds, just as it's supposed to.*"

"I don't understand."

"Naturally you don't. I realized at once that you had handed me a perfect situation the moment you attacked him. I'd been carrying that neat little truncheon with me for just such an occasion. I saw you look back, but you didn't see me in the trees. Once you were gone, I went to him, putting my arm around him and helping him to move farther away around the building. There was no one around, it was dark, so *carpe diem,* I seized the day."

He gave an exultant gasp. "It was so exciting, so *right.* I was surprised what little time it took. I got the truncheon ready, and, you know, Mike even said to me, *What is that?* Last thing he said. I hit him — hard, but not too hard — and he fell, then he got to his knees, and I helped him up, and slammed his head against the wall as hard as I could. Whack!"

Karfer clapped his hands together, and Carol jumped.

Exuberant, he went on. "Mike's head hitting

the wall sounded loud to me, but nobody heard. Blood came out of his ears, his eyes rolled up into his head, and I knew he was dying. I got him into the cover of the trees, and then I hurried to the dining hall and sat down at our table. I chatted to you, and all the time I knew he was out there dying, and you, my dear Carol, had been brought down, and you didn't know it yet."

The rain, an annoying mist until now, began to smack the windshield in large drops. Karfer leaned over and turned the wipers to high. He was bubbling with good humor, clearly happy to be able to explain to her how clever he had been.

"You were so obliging, Carol, telling Nikki about your scene with Mike. If you hadn't, I would have had to draw it out of you myself, not that it would have been difficult. I knew you'd have to boast about getting the best of a man."

Carol was taut, watching for a police car. She'd sideswipe it, then hope that Karfer had sense enough not to murder her in front of cops. She said, "Why did you bother to make Yench's death look like an accident if you wanted me to be implicated?"

"Ah, Carol, that's where you show your essential limitations. You don't have the imagination, the creativity, to plan and carry out something like this."

"But you do, Peter."

"The evidence is in front of you, but you can't see it. Mike dies, and it's maybe an accident, maybe not. Then just a few days later, Vertelle dies, and suddenly, it all points to you. Two men have conflict with you, and both die of head injuries. You might wiggle out of one, but not two murders. And the second one is a federal agent — that was deliberate on my part, so you get the death penalty for sure."

He let out a pleased sigh. "I wish I could have seen your face when you found the truncheon in with your makeup. I'd been in your room several times, looking around, checking your things."

"Jesus, Peter!" The thought of him pawing through her clothes was revolting to Carol.

"I figured," said Karfer, "that you wouldn't be using your makeup until the next day, so that's why I put the truncheon in that bag. It was a bit dicey planting it, and I had to wait around a bit, but it was worth the risk."

He peered through the wet windshield. "Our turnoff is coming up soon. Move over to the slow lane."

Carol's skin crawled. Off this main road, her chance to survive dropped close to zero. She had to keep his attention away from the traffic and on her. In a tone of disapproval she said, "You murdered two men just so you could bring me down?"

"Exactly. And you'd be hard put to convince me that the world isn't a much better place with those two bastards out of it."

"You didn't kill them to get at me, Peter; you did it because they made you feel small."

His good humor evaporated. The pressure of the gun in her side had been slack for the past few miles, but now he shoved it into her again. "Pricks, both of them," he snarled, "acting like they were so great. Ordering people around like servants." Resentment boiled in his voice. "I showed them."

Far ahead on the right side of the freeway she could see colored lights blinking. She squinted through the rain, hoping against hope that it was a patrol car. "I don't treat you that way, Peter," she said.

"You're worse. You're subtle. I've seen you smirk at me, thinking I didn't notice. Don't think I haven't noticed the sly digs you make at me, the way you laugh behind my back."

Carol's pulse jumped. It *was* a patrol car they were approaching, stopped behind another vehicle, probably someone speeding.

Knowing she had to keep him from looking ahead and seeing the cops, she said with a scornful laugh, "I thought you were smart, Peter, but you've shot yourself in the foot with this one."

He turned toward her, puzzled. "What are you talking about?"

"This. Kidnapping me. Your whole scheme was to have me found guilty of murder and executed, so you could enjoy the whole process, knowing you had masterminded it all. Now you've been seen by the security guard leaving the Academy with me. And then I disappear. How are you going to explain that?"

They were closing fast on the patrol car. *Please, God, let this work.*

Aloud she said, "You'll be a suspect in my death, and probably the others, too. You've really messed this one up, Peter."

He saw the patrol car just as Carol wrenched the wheel and stamped on the brakes. "You bitch!"

The car spun, skidding with squealing tires. The wheel bucked in Carol's hands.

Karfer, flung hard against the door, was yelling something, his mouth wide open as he raised the gun. Carol stared at the black mouth of the barrel.

Over his shoulder she had a glimpse of blinking lights, then they hit the patrol car side-on, metal tearing like foil, as the airbag exploded in front of her.

Almost simultaneously the sound of the shot split her head, the heat burning her cheek.

Then there was the chill of rain falling, the smell of steam, the feel of warm blood running down her face.

CHAPTER NINETEEN

Carol was in hospital a full day and night, and that was only because she was under observation for a head wound. Jill, arriving with an enormous basket of fruit, fussed over her, clucking at her injuries. "Hal says you can sue," she said.

"Sue whom?" said Carol. "I crashed the car deliberately."

"Well, of course this is America," said Jill. "Maybe the cops will sue *you*."

"What's happening with Michele Rackham?"

Jill plopped down on the metal chair beside Carol's bed. "She confessed. Hal, being Hal, wanted her to fight it, but Michele insisted."

"So why did she hire a hit man to kill her husband?"

"She wanted to hang on to what they'd got, and he wanted to take big risks and expand into the States. Michele told me, when she was holed up in our suite, how bitterly they'd fought over the issue. She was sure they'd lose everything they'd built up — there are investments and real estate all over the world — because of the confiscation laws in drug convictions. But Rackham wouldn't listen, so, as Michele said to me, she was forced to take drastic action."

After Jill had gone, Carol mused over Michele Rackham's decision to kill her husband, thinking sardonically that if she, herself, wanted someone murdered, she would do it with her own hands. Involving a paid killer almost always turned out to be a bad idea. If everything went successfully, you were still open to blackmail by the hit man or woman. If the killer were caught, then cutting a deal by turning state's evidence seemed the usual way to go.

It was definitely, Carol decided, a time when professional help was not the best option.

"You look like hell," said Leota cheerfully.

"I feel like hell." Carol was stiff and sore. She had two broken ribs, a superficial bullet wound that had necessitated shaving part of her scalp, and a peppering of powder burns on her face.

"Call me biased," said Leota, putting an arm around her. "But you still look awfully good to me."

She led Carol to her car, sitting blatantly in a Doctors Only section of the hospital's parking structure. "I've taken some days off to play Florence Nightingale with you," Leota said, opening the door and easing Carol into the vehicle. "And I've tidied my apartment in your honor."

Carol smiled at her with gentle mockery. "Good grief. You can leave the Rackham case that long?"

Leota slid behind the wheel. "I think my name is well-established there," she said. "I'm thinking of moving on to the Peter Karfer case next."

Carol's smile faded. "Will the federal prosecutor be asking for the death penalty?"

Execution had been banned in Australia for many years, and Carol had never seen any of the murderers she'd arrested die for their crimes.

Leota said with satisfaction. "Absolutely."

"But he's mad, Leota. He isn't fully responsible."

Leota leaned across and patted Carol's knee. "What was mad," she said, "was taking you on. I'd say he was positively insane to try it!"

UNDER SUSPICION by Claire McNab. 224 pp. 12th Detective
Inspector Carol Ashton mystery.   ISBN 1-56280-261-5 $11.95

UNFORGETTABLE by Karin Kallmaker. 288 pp. Can each
woman win her true love's heart?   ISBN 1-56280-260-7   11.95

MURDER UNDERCOVER by Claire McNab. 192 pp. 1st Denise
Cleever thriller.   ISBN 1-56280-259-3   11.95

EVERYTIME WE SAY GOODBYE by Jaye Maiman. 272 pp.
7th Robin Miller mystery.   ISBN 1-56280-248-8   11.95

SEVENTH HEAVEN by Kate Calloway. 240 pp. 7th Cassidy
James mystery.   ISBN 1-56280-262-3   11.95

STRANGERS IN THE NIGHT by Barbara Johnson. 208 pp. Her
body and soul react to a stranger's touch.   ISBN 1-56280-256-9   11.95

THE VERY THOUGHT OF YOU edited by Barbara Grier and
Christine Cassidy. 288 pp. Erotic love stories by Naiad Press
authors.   ISBN 1-56280-250-X   14.95

TO HAVE AND TO HOLD by PeGGy J. Herring. 192 pp. Their
friendship grows to intense passion . . .   ISBN 1-56280-251-8   11.95

INTIMATE STRANGER by Laura DeHart Young. 192 pp.
Ignoring Tray's myserious past, could Cole be playing with fire?
                                               ISBN 1-56280-249-6   11.95

SHATTERED ILLUSIONS by Kaye Davis. 256 pp. 4th
Maris Middleton mystery.   ISBN 1-56280-252-6   11.95

SET UP by Claire McNab. 224 pp. 11th Detective Inspector Carol
Ashton mystery.   ISBN 1-56280-255-0   11.95

THE DAWNING by Laura Adams. 224 pp. What if you had the
power to change the past?   ISBN 1-56280-246-1   11.95

NEVER ENDING by Marianne K. Martin. 224 pp. Temptation
appears in the form of an old friend and lover. ISBN 1-56280-247-X   11.95

ONE OF OUR OWN by Diane Salvatore. 240 pp. Carly Matson
has a secret. So does Lela Johns.   ISBN 1-56280-243-7   11.95

DOUBLE TAKEOUT by Tracey Richardson. 176 pp. 3rd Stevie
Houston mystery.   ISBN 1-56280-244-5   11.95

CAPTIVE HEART by Frankie J. Jones. 176 pp. Love in the
fast lane or heartside romance?   ISBN 1-56280-258-5   11.95

WICKED GOOD TIME by Diana Tremain Braund. 224 pp. In
charge at work, out of control in her heart.   ISBN 1-56280-241-0   11.95

SNAKE EYES by Pat Welch. 256 pp. 7th Helen Black mystery.
                                                     ISBN 1-56280-242-9   11.95

CHANGE OF HEART by Linda Hill. 176 pp. High fashion and
love in a glamorous world.   ISBN 1-56280-238-0   11.95

UNSTRUNG HEART by Robbi Sommers. 176 pp. Putting life
in order again.   ISBN 1-56280-239-9   11.95

BIRDS OF A FEATHER by Jackie Calhoun. 240 pp. Life begins
with love.   ISBN 1-56280-240-2   11.95

THE DRIVE by Trisha Todd. 176 pp. The star of *Claire of the
Moon* tells all!   ISBN 1-56280-237-2   11.95

BOTH SIDES by Saxon Bennett. 240 pp. A community of
women falling in and out of love.   ISBN 1-56280-236-4   11.95

WATERMARK by Karin Kallmaker. 256 pp. One burning
question . . . how to lead her back to love?   ISBN 1-56280-235-6   11.95

THE OTHER WOMAN by Ann O'Leary. 240 pp. Her roguish
way draws women like a magnet.   ISBN 1-56280-234-8   11.95

SILVER THREADS by Lyn Denison.208 pp. Finding her way
back to love . . .   ISBN 1-56280-231-3   11.95

CHIMNEY ROCK BLUES by Janet McClellan. 224 pp. 4th Tru
North mystery.   ISBN 1-56280-233-X   11.95

OMAHA'S BELL by Penny Hayes. 208 pp. Orphaned Keeley
Delaney woos the lovely Prudence Morris.   ISBN 1-56280-232-1   11.95

SIXTH SENSE by Kate Calloway. 224 pp. 6th Cassidy James
mystery.   ISBN 1-56280-228-3   11.95

DAWN OF THE DANCE by Marianne K. Martin. 224 pp. A dance
with an old friend, nothing more . . . yeah!   ISBN 1-56280-229-1   11.95

THOSE WHO WAIT by Peggy J. Herring. 160 pp. Two
sisters . . . in love with the same woman.   ISBN 1-56280-223-2   11.95

WHISPERS IN THE WIND by Frankie J. Jones. 192 pp. "If you
don't want this," she whispered, "all you have to say is 'stop.' "
                                                     ISBN 1-56280-226-7   11.95

WHEN SOME BODY DISAPPEARS by Therese Szymanski.
192 pp. 3rd Brett Higgins mystery.   ISBN 1-56280-227-5   11.95

UNTIL THE END by Kaye Davis. 256pp. 3rd Maris Middleton
mystery.   ISBN 1-56280-222-4   11.95

FIFTH WHEEL by Kate Calloway. 224 pp. 5th Cassidy James
mystery.   ISBN 1-56280-218-6   11.95

JUST YESTERDAY by Linda Hill. 176 pp. Reliving all the
passion of yesterday.   ISBN 1-56280-219-4   11.95

THE TOUCH OF YOUR HAND edited by Barbara Grier and
Christine Cassidy. 304 pp. Erotic love stories by Naiad Press
authors.   ISBN 1-56280-220-8   14.95

WINDROW GARDEN by Janet McClellan. 192 pp. They discover
a passion they never dreamed possible.   ISBN 1-56280-216-X   11.95

PAST DUE by Claire McNab. 224 pp. 10th Carol Ashton
mystery.   ISBN 1-56280-217-8   11.95

CHRISTABEL by Laura Adams. 224 pp. Two captive hearts and
the passion that will set them free.   ISBN 1-56280-214-3   11.95

PRIVATE PASSIONS by Laura DeHart Young. 192 pp. An
unforgettable new portrait of lesbian love . . .   ISBN 1-56280-215-1   11.95

BAD MOON RISING by Barbara Johnson. 208 pp. 2nd Colleen
Fitzgerald mystery.   ISBN 1-56280-211-9   11.95

RIVER QUAY by Janet McClellan. 208 pp. 3rd Tru North
mystery.   ISBN 1-56280-212-7   11.95

ENDLESS LOVE by Lisa Shapiro. 272 pp. To believe, once
again, that love can be forever.   ISBN 1-56280-213-5   11.95

FALLEN FROM GRACE by Pat Welch. 256 pp. 6th Helen Black
mystery.   ISBN 1-56280-209-7   11.95

THE NAKED EYE by Catherine Ennis. 208 pp. Her lover in the
camera's eye . . .   ISBN 1-56280-210-0   11.95

OVER THE LINE by Tracey Richardson. 176 pp. 2nd Stevie
Houston mystery.   ISBN 1-56280-202-X   11.95

JULIA'S SONG by Ann O'Leary. 208 pp. Strangely
disturbing . . . strangely exciting.   ISBN 1-56280-197-X   11.95

LOVE IN THE BALANCE by Marianne K. Martin. 256 pp.
Weighing the costs of love . . .   ISBN 1-56280-199-6   11.95

PIECE OF MY HEART by Julia Watts. 208 pp. All the
stuff that dreams are made of —   ISBN 1-56280-206-2   11.95

MAKING UP FOR LOST TIME by Karin Kallmaker. 240 pp.
Nobody does it better . . .   ISBN 1-56280-196-1   11.95

GOLD FEVER by Lyn Denison. 224 pp. By author of *Dream
Lover.*   ISBN 1-56280-201-1   11.95

WHEN THE DEAD SPEAK by Therese Szymanski. 224 pp. 2nd
Brett Higgins mystery.   ISBN 1-56280-198-8   11.95

FOURTH DOWN by Kate Calloway. 240 pp. 4th Cassidy James
mystery.   ISBN 1-56280-193-7   11.95

A MOMENT'S INDISCRETION by Peggy J. Herring. 176 pp.
There's a fine line between love and lust . . .   ISBN 1-56280-194-5   11.95

CITY LIGHTS COUNTRY CANDLES by Penny Hayes. 208 pp.
About the women she has known . . .   ISBN 1-56280-195-3   11.95

POSSESSIONS by Kaye Davis. 240 pp. 2nd Maris Middleton
mystery.   ISBN 1-56280-192-9   11.95

A QUESTION OF LOVE by Saxon Bennett. 208 pp. Every
woman is granted one great love.   ISBN 1-56280-205-4   11.95

RHYTHM TIDE by Frankie J. Jones. 160 pp. . . . to desire
passionately and be passionately desired.   ISBN 1-56280-189-9   11.95

PENN VALLEY PHOENIX by Janet McClellan. 208 pp. 2nd
Tru North Mystery.   ISBN 1-56280-200-3   11.95

OLD BLACK MAGIC by Jaye Maiman. 272 pp. 6th Robin
Miller mystery.   ISBN 1-56280-175-9   11.95

LEGACY OF LOVE by Marianne K. Martin. 240 pp. Women
will do anything for her . . .   ISBN 1-56280-184-8   11.95

LETTING GO by Ann O'Leary. 160 pp. Laura, at 39, in love
with 23-year-old Kate.   ISBN 1-56280-183-X   11.95

LADY BE GOOD edited by Barbara Grier and Christine Cassidy.
288 pp. Erotic stories by Naiad Press authors. ISBN 1-56280-180-5   14.95

CHAIN LETTER by Claire McNab. 288 pp. 9th Carol Ashton
mystery.   ISBN 1-56280-181-3   11.95

NIGHT VISION by Laura Adams. 256 pp. Erotic fantasy romance
by "famous" author.   ISBN 1-56280-182-1   11.95

SEA TO SHINING SEA by Lisa Shapiro. 256 pp. Unable to resist
the raging passion . . .   ISBN 1-56280-177-5   11.95

THIRD DEGREE by Kate Calloway. 224 pp. 3rd Cassidy James
mystery.   ISBN 1-56280-185-6   11.95

WHEN THE DANCING STOPS by Therese Szymanski. 272 pp.
1st Brett Higgins mystery.   ISBN 1-56280-186-4   11.95

PHASES OF THE MOON by Julia Watts. 192 pp. . . . . . hungry
for everything life has to offer.   ISBN 1-56280-176-7   11.95

BABY IT'S COLD by Jaye Maiman. 256 pp. 5th Robin Miller
mystery.   ISBN 1-56280-156-2   10.95

CLASS REUNION by Linda Hill. 176 pp. The girl from her
past . . .   ISBN 1-56280-178-3   11.95

DREAM LOVER by Lyn Denison. 224 pp. A soft, sensuous,
romantic fantasy.   ISBN 1-56280-173-2   11.95

FORTY LOVE by Diana Simmonds. 288 pp. Joyous, heart-
warming romance.   ISBN 1-56280-171-6   11.95

IN THE MOOD by Robbi Sommers. 160 pp. The queen of
erotic tension! ISBN 1-56280-172-4　　11.95

SWIMMING CAT COVE by Lauren Wright Douglas. 192 pp. 2nd
Allison O'Neil Mystery. ISBN 1-56280-168-6　　11.95

THE LOVING LESBIAN by Claire McNab and Sharon Gedan.
240 pp. Explore the experiences that make lesbian love unique.
ISBN 1-56280-169-4　　14.95

COURTED by Celia Cohen. 160 pp. Sparkling romantic
encounter. ISBN 1-56280-166-X　　11.95

SEASONS OF THE HEART by Jackie Calhoun. 240 pp. Romance
through the years. ISBN 1-56280-167-8　　11.95

K. C. BOMBER by Janet McClellan. 208 pp. 1st Tru North
mystery. ISBN 1-56280-157-0　　11.95

LAST RITES by Tracey Richardson. 192 pp. 1st Stevie Houston
mystery. ISBN 1-56280-164-3　　11.95

EMBRACE IN MOTION by Karin Kallmaker. 256 pp. A whirlwind
love affair. ISBN 1-56280-165-1　　11.95

HOT CHECK by Peggy J. Herring. 192 pp. Will workaholic Alice
fall for guitarist Ricky? ISBN 1-56280-163-5　　11.95

OLD TIES by Saxon Bennett. 176 pp. Can Cleo surrender to a
passionate new love? ISBN 1-56280-159-7　　11.95

LOVE ON THE LINE by Laura DeHart Young. 176 pp. Will Stef
win Kay's heart? ISBN 1-56280-162-7　　11.95

DEVIL'S LEG CROSSING by Kaye Davis. 192 pp. 1st Maris
Middleton mystery. ISBN 1-56280-158-9　　11.95

COSTA BRAVA by Marta Balletbo-Coll. 144 pp. Read the book,
see the movie! ISBN 1-56280-160-0　　11.95

MEETING MAGDALENE & OTHER STORIES by
Marilyn Freeman. 144 pp. Read the book, see the movie!
ISBN 1-56280-170-8　　11.95

SECOND FIDDLE by Kate Kalloway. 208 pp. 2nd P.I. Cassidy James
mystery. ISBN 1-56280-161-9　　11.95

LAUREL by Isabel Miller. 128 pp. By the author of the beloved
Patience and Sarah. ISBN 1-56280-146-5　　10.95

LOVE OR MONEY by Jackie Calhoun. 240 pp. The romance of
real life. ISBN 1-56280-147-3　　10.95

SMOKE AND MIRRORS by Pat Welch. 224 pp. 5th Helen Black
Mystery. ISBN 1-56280-143-0　　10.95

DANCING IN THE DARK edited by Barbara Grier & Christine
Cassidy. 272 pp. Erotic love stories by Naiad Press authors.
ISBN 1-56280-144-9　　14.95

TIME AND TIME AGAIN by Catherine Ennis. 176 pp. Passionate
love affair.   ISBN 1-56280-145-7   10.95

PAXTON COURT by Diane Salvatore. 256 pp. Erotic and wickedly
funny contemporary tale about the business of learning to live
together.   ISBN 1-56280-114-7   10.95

INNER CIRCLE by Claire McNab. 208 pp. 8th Carol Ashton
Mystery.   ISBN 1-56280-135-X   11.95

LESBIAN SEX: AN ORAL HISTORY by Susan Johnson.
240 pp. Need we say more?   ISBN 1-56280-142-2   14.95

WILD THINGS by Karin Kallmaker. 240 pp. By the undisputed
mistress of lesbian romance.   ISBN 1-56280-139-2   11.95

THE GIRL NEXT DOOR by Mindy Kaplan. 208 pp. Just what
you'd expect.   ISBN 1-56280-140-6   11.95

NOW AND THEN by Penny Hayes. 240 pp. Romance on the
westward journey.   ISBN 1-56280-121-X   11.95

HEART ON FIRE by Diana Simmonds. 176 pp. The romantic and
erotic rival of *Curious Wine*.   ISBN 1-56280-152-X   11.95

DEATH AT LAVENDER BAY by Lauren Wright Douglas. 208 pp.
1st Allison O'Neil Mystery.   ISBN 1-56280-085-X   11.95

YES I SAID YES I WILL by Judith McDaniel. 272 pp. Hot
romance by famous author.   ISBN 1-56280-138-4   11.95

FORBIDDEN FIRES by Margaret C. Anderson. Edited by Mathilda
Hills. 176 pp. Famous author's "unpublished" Lesbian romance.
                                                ISBN 1-56280-123-6   21.95

SIDE TRACKS by Teresa Stores. 160 pp. Gender-bending
Lesbians on the road.   ISBN 1-56280-122-8   10.95

WILDWOOD FLOWERS by Julia Watts. 208 pp. Hilarious and
heart-warming tale of true love.   ISBN 1-56280-127-9   10.95

NEVER SAY NEVER by Linda Hill. 224 pp. Rule #1: Never get
involved with . . .   ISBN 1-56280-126-0   11.95

THE WISH LIST by Saxon Bennett. 192 pp. Romance through
the years.   ISBN 1-56280-125-2   10.95

OUT OF THE NIGHT by Kris Bruyer. 192 pp. Spine-tingling
thriller.   ISBN 1-56280-120-1   10.95

FAMILY SECRETS by Laura DeHart Young. 208 pp. Enthralling
romance and suspense.   ISBN 1-56280-119-8   10.95

INLAND PASSAGE by Jane Rule. 288 pp. Tales exploring conven-
tional & unconventional relationships.   ISBN 0-930044-56-8   10.95

DOUBLE BLUFF by Claire McNab. 208 pp. 7th Carol Ashton
Mystery.   ISBN 1-56280-096-5   11.95

BAR GIRLS by Lauran Hoffman. 176 pp. See the movie, read
the book!   ISBN 1-56280-115-5   10.95

THE FIRST TIME EVER edited by Barbara Grier & Christine Cassidy. 272 pp. Love stories by Naiad Press authors.
ISBN 1-56280-086-8   14.95

MISS PETTIBONE AND MISS McGRAW by Brenda Weathers. 208 pp. A charming ghostly love story.   ISBN 1-56280-151-1   10.95

CHANGES by Jackie Calhoun. 208 pp. Involved romance and relationships.   ISBN 1-56280-083-3   10.95

FAIR PLAY by Rose Beecham. 256 pp. An Amanda Valentine Mystery.   ISBN 1-56280-081-7   10.95

PAYBACK by Celia Cohen. 176 pp. A gripping thriller of romance, revenge and betrayal.   ISBN 1-56280-084-1   10.95

THE BEACH AFFAIR by Barbara Johnson. 224 pp. Sizzling summer romance/mystery/intrigue.   ISBN 1-56280-090-6   10.95

GETTING THERE by Robbi Sommers. 192 pp. Nobody does it like Robbi!   ISBN 1-56280-099-X   10.95

FINAL CUT by Lisa Haddock. 208 pp. 2nd Carmen Ramirez Mystery.   ISBN 1-56280-088-4   10.95

FLASHPOINT by Katherine V. Forrest. 256 pp. A Lesbian blockbuster!   ISBN 1-56280-079-5   10.95

CLAIRE OF THE MOON by Nicole Conn. Audio Book — Read by Marianne Hyatt.   ISBN 1-56280-113-9   13.95

FOR LOVE AND FOR LIFE: INTIMATE PORTRAITS OF LESBIAN COUPLES by Susan Johnson. 224 pp.
ISBN 1-56280-091-4   14.95

DEVOTION by Mindy Kaplan. 192 pp. See the movie — read the book!   ISBN 1-56280-093-0   10.95

SOMEONE TO WATCH by Jaye Maiman. 272 pp. 4th Robin Miller Mystery.   ISBN 1-56280-095-7   10.95

GREENER THAN GRASS by Jennifer Fulton. 208 pp. A young woman — a stranger in her bed.   ISBN 1-56280-092-2   10.95

TRAVELS WITH DIANA HUNTER by Regine Sands. Erotic lesbian romp. Audio Book (2 cassettes)   ISBN 1-56280-107-4   13.95

CABIN FEVER by Carol Schmidt. 256 pp. Sizzling suspense and passion.   ISBN 1-56280-089-1   10.95

THERE WILL BE NO GOODBYES by Laura DeHart Young. 192 pp. Romantic love, strength, and friendship.   ISBN 1-56280-103-1   10.95

FAULTLINE by Sheila Ortiz Taylor. 144 pp. Joyous comic lesbian novel.   ISBN 1-56280-108-2   9.95

OPEN HOUSE by Pat Welch. 176 pp. 4th Helen Black Mystery.
ISBN 1-56280-102-3   10.95

ONCE MORE WITH FEELING by Peggy J. Herring. 240 pp. Lighthearted, loving romantic adventure.   ISBN 1-56280-089-2   11.95

WHISPERS by Kris Bruyer. 176 pp. Romantic ghost story.
ISBN 1-56280-082-5   10.95

PAINTED MOON by Karin Kallmaker. 224 pp. Delicious
Kallmaker romance.   ISBN 1-56280-075-2   11.95

THE MYSTERIOUS NAIAD edited by Katherine V. Forrest &
Barbara Grier. 320 pp. Love stories by Naiad Press authors.
ISBN 1-56280-074-4   14.95

DAUGHTERS OF A CORAL DAWN by Katherine V. Forrest.
240 pp. Tenth Anniversay Edition.   ISBN 1-56280-104-X   11.95

BODY GUARD by Claire McNab. 208 pp. 6th Carol Ashton
Mystery.   ISBN 1-56280-073-6   11.95

CACTUS LOVE by Lee Lynch. 192 pp. Stories by the beloved
storyteller.   ISBN 1-56280-071-X   9.95

SECOND GUESS by Rose Beecham. 216 pp. An Amanda
Valentine Mystery.   ISBN 1-56280-069-8   9.95

A RAGE OF MAIDENS by Lauren Wright Douglas. 240 pp.
6th Caitlin Reece Mystery.   ISBN 1-56280-068-X   10.95

TRIPLE EXPOSURE by Jackie Calhoun. 224 pp. Romantic
drama involving many characters.   ISBN 1-56280-067-1   10.95

PERSONAL ADS by Robbi Sommers. 176 pp. Sizzling short
stories.   ISBN 1-56280-059-0   11.95

CROSSWORDS by Penny Sumner. 256 pp. 2nd Victoria Cross
Mystery.   ISBN 1-56280-064-7   9.95

SWEET CHERRY WINE by Carol Schmidt. 224 pp. A novel of
suspense.   ISBN 1-56280-063-9   9.95

CERTAIN SMILES by Dorothy Tell. 160 pp. Erotic short stories.
ISBN 1-56280-066-3   9.95

EDITED OUT by Lisa Haddock. 224 pp. 1st Carmen Ramirez
Mystery.   ISBN 1-56280-077-9   9.95

SMOKEY O by Celia Cohen. 176 pp. Relationships on the
playing field.   ISBN 1-56280-057-4   9.95

KATHLEEN O'DONALD by Penny Hayes. 256 pp. Rose and
Kathleen find each other and employment in 1909 NYC.
ISBN 1-56280-070-1   9.95

STAYING HOME by Elisabeth Nonas. 256 pp. Molly and Alix
want a baby . . . or do they?   ISBN 1-56280-076-0   10.95

TRUE LOVE by Jennifer Fulton. 240 pp. Six lesbians searching
for love in all the "right" places.   ISBN 1-56280-035-3   11.95

THE ROMANTIC NAIAD edited by Katherine V. Forrest &
Barbara Grier. 336 pp. Love stories by Naiad Press authors.
ISBN 1-56280-054-X   14.95

UNDER MY SKIN by Jaye Maiman. 336 pp. 3rd Robin Miller
Mystery.   ISBN 1-56280-049-3.   11.95

CAR POOL by Karin Kallmaker. 272pp. Lesbians on wheels
and then some!   ISBN 1-56280-048-5   11.95

NOT TELLING MOTHER: STORIES FROM A LIFE by Diane
Salvatore. 176 pp. Her 3rd novel.   ISBN 1-56280-044-2   9.95

GOBLIN MARKET by Lauren Wright Douglas. 240pp. 5th Caitlin
Reece Mystery.   ISBN 1-56280-047-7   10.95

BEHIND CLOSED DOORS by Robbi Sommers. 192 pp. Hot,
erotic short stories.   ISBN 1-56280-039-6   11.95

CLAIRE OF THE MOON by Nicole Conn. 192 pp. See the
movie — read the book!   ISBN 1-56280-038-8   11.95

SILENT HEART by Claire McNab. 192 pp. Exotic Lesbian
romance.   ISBN 1-56280-036-1   11.95

SAVING GRACE by Jennifer Fulton. 240 pp. Adventure and
romantic entanglement.   ISBN 1-56280-051-5   11.95

CURIOUS WINE by Katherine V. Forrest. 176 pp. Tenth Anniversary Edition. The most popular contemporary Lesbian love story.
                                                ISBN 1-56280-053-1   11.95
        Audio Book (2 cassettes)   ISBN 1-56280-105-8   13.95

A PROPER BURIAL by Pat Welch. 192 pp. 3rd Helen Black
Mystery.   ISBN 1-56280-033-7   9.95

SILVERLAKE HEAT: A Novel of Suspense by Carol Schmidt.
240 pp. Rhonda is as hot as Laney's dreams.   ISBN 1-56280-031-0   9.95

LOVE, ZENA BETH by Diane Salvatore. 224 pp. The most talked
about lesbian novel of the nineties!   ISBN 1-56280-030-2   10.95

A DOORYARD FULL OF FLOWERS by Isabel Miller. 160 pp.
Stories incl. 2 sequels to *Patience and Sarah*.   ISBN 1-56280-029-9   9.95

MURDER BY TRADITION by Katherine V. Forrest. 288 pp. 4th
Kate Delafield Mystery.   ISBN 1-56280-002-7   11.95

THE EROTIC NAIAD edited by Katherine V. Forrest & Barbara
Grier. 224 pp. Love stories by Naiad Press authors.
                                                ISBN 1-56280-026-4   14.95

DEAD CERTAIN by Claire McNab. 224 pp. 5th Carol Ashton
Mystery.   ISBN 1-56280-027-2   11.95

CRAZY FOR LOVING by Jaye Maiman. 320 pp. 2nd Robin Miller
Mystery.   ISBN 1-56280-025-6   11.95

UNCERTAIN COMPANIONS by Robbi Sommers. 204 pp.
Steamy, erotic novel.   ISBN 1-56280-017-5   11.95

A TIGER'S HEART by Lauren Wright Douglas. 240 pp. 4th Caitlin
Reece Mystery.   ISBN 1-56280-018-3   9.95

PAPERBACK ROMANCE by Karin Kallmaker. 256 pp. A
delicious romance.   ISBN 1-56280-019-1   11.95

THE LAVENDER HOUSE MURDER by Nikki Baker. 224 pp.
2nd Virginia Kelly Mystery.   ISBN 1-56280-012-4   9.95

PASSION BAY by Jennifer Fulton. 224 pp. Passionate romance,
virgin beaches, tropical skies.   ISBN 1-56280-028-0   11.95

STICKS AND STONES by Jackie Calhoun. Contemporary
lesbian lives and loves.
Audio Book (2 cassettes)   ISBN 1-56280-106-6   13.95

UNDER THE SOUTHERN CROSS by Claire McNab. 192 pp.
Romantic nights Down Under.   ISBN 1-56280-011-6   11.95

GRASSY FLATS by Penny Hayes. 256 pp. Lesbian romance in
the '30s.   ISBN 1-56280-010-8   9.95

THE END OF APRIL by Penny Sumner. 240 pp. 1st Victoria
Cross Mystery.   ISBN 1-56280-007-8   8.95

KISS AND TELL by Robbi Sommers. 192 pp. Scorching stories
by the author of *Pleasures*.   ISBN 1-56280-005-1   11.95

IN THE GAME by Nikki Baker. 192 pp. 1st Virginia Kelly
Mystery.   ISBN 1-56280-004-3   9.95

STRANDED by Camarin Grae. 320 pp. Entertaining, riveting
adventure.   ISBN 0-941483-99-1   9.95

THE DAUGHTERS OF ARTEMIS by Lauren Wright Douglas.
240 pp. 3rd Caitlin Reece Mystery.   ISBN 0-941483-95-9   9.95

THE HALLELUJAH MURDERS by Dorothy Tell. 176 pp. 2nd
Poppy Dillworth Mystery.   ISBN 0-941483-88-6   8.95

BENEDICTION by Diane Salvatore. 272 pp. Striking, contemporary romantic novel.   ISBN 0-941483-90-8   11.95

TOUCHWOOD by Karin Kallmaker. 240 pp. Loving, May/
December romance.   ISBN 0-941483-76-2   11.95

COP OUT by Claire McNab. 208 pp. 4th Carol Ashton Mystery.

                                             ISBN 0-941483-84-3   10.95

THE BEVERLY MALIBU by Katherine V. Forrest. 288 pp. 3rd
Kate Delafield Mystery.   ISBN 0-941483-48-7   11.95

I LEFT MY HEART by Jaye Maiman. 320 pp. 1st Robin Miller
Mystery.   ISBN 0-941483-72-X   11.95

THE PRICE OF SALT by Patricia Highsmith (writing as Claire
Morgan). 288 pp. Classic lesbian novel, first issued in 1952 . . .
acknowledged by its author under her own, very famous, name.
                                             ISBN 1-56280-003-5   12.95

SIDE BY SIDE by Isabel Miller. 256 pp. From beloved author of
Patience and Sarah.   ISBN 0-941483-77-0   9.95

STAYING POWER: LONG TERM LESBIAN COUPLES by
Susan E. Johnson. 352 pp. Joys of coupledom. ISBN 0-941483-75-4   14.95

SLICK by Camarin Grae. 304 pp. Exotic, erotic adventure.
ISBN 0-941483-74-6   9.95

NINTH LIFE by Lauren Wright Douglas. 256 pp. 2nd Caitlin
Reece Mystery.   ISBN 0-941483-50-9   9.95

PLAYERS by Robbi Sommers. 192 pp. Sizzling, erotic novel.
ISBN 0-941483-73-8   9.95

MURDER AT RED ROOK RANCH by Dorothy Tell. 224 pp.
1st Poppy Dillworth Mystery.   ISBN 0-941483-80-0   8.95

A ROOM FULL OF WOMEN by Elisabeth Nonas. 256 pp.
Contemporary Lesbian lives.   ISBN 0-941483-69-X   9.95

THEME FOR DIVERSE INSTRUMENTS by Jane Rule. 208 pp.
Powerful romantic lesbian stories.   ISBN 0-941483-63-0   8.95

DEATH DOWN UNDER by Claire McNab. 240 pp. 3rd Carol
Ashton Mystery.   ISBN 0-941483-39-8   11.95

THERE'S SOMETHING I'VE BEEN MEANING TO TELL YOU
Ed. by Loralee MacPike. 288 pp. Gay men and lesbians coming out
to their children.   ISBN 0-941483-44-4   9.95

LIFTING BELLY by Gertrude Stein. Ed. by Rebecca Mark. 104 pp.
Erotic poetry.   ISBN 0-941483-51-7   10.95

AFTER THE FIRE by Jane Rule. 256 pp. Warm, human novel by
this incomparable author.   ISBN 0-941483-45-2   8.95

PLEASURES by Robbi Sommers. 204 pp. Unprecedented
eroticism.   ISBN 0-941483-49-5   11.95

EDGEWISE by Camarin Grae. 372 pp. Spellbinding
adventure.   ISBN 0-941483-19-3   9.95

FATAL REUNION by Claire McNab. 224 pp. 2nd Carol Ashton
Mystery.   ISBN 0-941483-40-1   11.95

IN EVERY PORT by Karin Kallmaker. 228 pp. Jessica's sexy,
adventuresome travels.   ISBN 0-941483-34-7   11.95

OF LOVE AND GLORY by Evelyn Kennedy. 192 pp. Exciting
WWII romance.   ISBN 0-941483-32-0   10.95

CLICKING STONES by Nancy Tyler Glenn. 288 pp. Love
transcending time.   ISBN 0-941483-31-2   9.95

These are just a few of the many Naiad Press titles — we are the oldest and
largest lesbian/feminist publishing company in the world. We also offer an
enormous selection of lesbian video products. Please request a complete
catalog. We offer personal service; we encourage and welcome direct mail
orders from individuals who have limited access to bookstores carrying our
publications.

LOOKING FOR NAIAD?

Buy our books at
www.naiadpress.com

or call our toll-free number
1-800-533-1973

or by fax (24 hours a day)
1-850-539-9731